Dick Dona

CRASH
and other
STORIES

First Limited Edition

Published by D-Zine/Lulu Publishers

First published as a collection 2013

by Dick Donaghue/Lulu Enterprises, Inc.

ISBN: 978-1-291-33203-2
Content ID: 13672169

Book Title: CRASH AND OTHER STORIES

In Memory of Mary Hellion Shelly

Friend and Editor.

***

By the same author

Dance Of The Mocking Birds (Novel)

Published by TAF Publishing Dublin.

ISBN 978-1907522-17-8

Marja van Kampen

"**A Determined Life In Art**" (Biography)

Published by The Book Producers, Dublin. 2011

ISBN 978-1-908417-21-3

Table of contents

ENIGMA

I'm walking home from work, up Friar's Hill, where I live near the top. It's a steady half-hour walk from the office but I've stopped using the car since the doctor advised me to get more exercise.

The setting sun has turned scattered clouds a deep red and I'm enjoying the last warm rays on my face. The trees along this stretch of the road smell dry and brittle. Another scorcher is expected tomorrow. Today was a long hot slog at the office between heavy meetings and awkward questions. Now I'm looking forward to a quiet drink at home with my feet up and then a good night's sleep.

I see a man coming towards me and it seems as if he is walking straight out of the sun. As he comes closer his silhouetted shape becomes familiar then recognizable. Something between shock and amazement stops me dead in my tracks. This man is my father. I can hardly believe what I'm seeing. Can it be, I wonder, that the glowing red sky coupled with weariness are causing my eyes to play tricks on me? I shake myself and stare at the figure, haloed in sunlight, still moving towards me. There's no mistake. It's my father right enough. My father who's been dead these twenty years.

My heart misses a full beat and the breath catches in my throat. Stumbling against the wall, as my legs give way, I push hard against the rough stones to right myself. I just can't believe what I'm seeing.

"Hello, Micileen," he says, greeting me with a smile and using the Gaelic version of my name - *'Little Michael'* - as he always did during his lifetime. He grasps my hand firmly and its warmth brings me back to childhood. I can feel tears welling in my eyes

"You look tired," he says, head tilted back, scrutinizing my face. My father is a short man, a head smaller than me, but his broad shoulders give him a strong solid stance.

"Pop," is all I can say. So glad to see him; to touch him again. But I still can't believe that, on this warm evening, I'm standing here with the father who reared me with singular affection and taught me everything I know in business.

Then I recognize the dream. It's the same one I have whenever the pressures of business weigh me down like an over-loaded old fruit tree. That's when my father appears and we talk things over in the quiet logical way he had about him. He smiles his way through the problems as if business was only some game to be toyed with and enjoyed.

When he died twenty years ago I inherited the company. Everything ran smoothly for a while until Japanese competition increased. Then, as things got tougher, the dreams started. When the pressures got me down and I couldn't untangle myself from a knot of worries he'd come to me, in my sleep, and help unravel them. The following morning I'd wake with a clear head and renewed energy. My staff, in turn, responded with fresh ideas and strategies that gradually nudged the sales graph back up again. And the dream was forgotten until the next crisis.

"Pop." I stammer again, launching into a tale of woe about today's strenuous meetings with the sales department. Business has never been so bad. It's as if our market has suddenly shrunk. We've had to discontinue three of our best lines because we can no longer produce them at competitive prices. And it looks like we'll have to take one or two reps off the road. Cut-backs all round seem to be the only way out of this mess.

Back in my own office, surrounded by sheaves of paper recording the plummeting sales figures, insufficient Autumn budget, and the Bank's warnings about future borrowing, I felt totally alone and disheartened. The future looks bleak and for the first time I'm considering selling the company, for whatever I can get, and retiring. At least the house is my own and I won't starve. I'm getting too tired for these weighty problems and there's no-one to take on the burden of my desk. I never married and have no heirs. Sometimes I wonder if I ever had the aptitude for the manufacturing business. Maybe what it needs now is a younger, fresher, approach.

Like a lost child I shamefully blurt all this out to my father. The business he single handedly founded, nurtured, expanded, and passed on to me, has come to this.

He listens quietly, head slightly to one side, lips pursed. I wait dejectedly for his wise words. He's still holding my hand and, as I feel his energy running into me like a warm stream, I begin to relax. I'm happy to simply stand here with him and wait for advice but now his look changes and he seems to be gazing beyond me at some distant object.

"There's someone I would like you to meet," he says. "Someone you never met before." He pauses, watching my reaction, a soft glow fills his eyes. This is a new shift in the dream. I wonder what he means. Will he introduce me to some new person who I will employ and bring into the firm? Someone who will change the course of these present downward sales trends?

He laughs softly as if reading my jumbled thoughts. "No," he says. "Let's forget business for the moment. This is more important. This is a beautiful wee woman who you know but sadly have never seen. Her name is Kathleen." His face spreads in a wide smile as he watches my puzzled expression, "Your mother."

A great gush of emotion erupts inside my chest and threatens to throw me to the ground. My mother died when I was born. I feel the warm stones under my hand as I reach to steady myself again.

"Are you all right Mr. O'Sullivan?" a voice filters through to me. A car has pulled up and a young man, whom I recognize as my new neighbour from the top of the hill, is leaning across the passenger seat and peering at me. "Can I give you a lift?"

I indicate my father to him, and that we are talking, but I realize that he is not aware of the dream so I make a walking gesture with my fingers. "For the good of my health," I call out. He nods, sympathetically, and drives off.

The sun, down behind the hill now, is throwing my father into silhouette. It's difficult for me to make out his face. He continues as if there had been no interruption. "She's waited a long time Micileen," he says fondly. "Over sixty years," he adds, shaking his head slowly as if reading my thoughts.

I sorely want to discuss business with him, but yes, I want to meet my mother too, even if it is only in a dream. My father's voice, though still soft, is full of urgency and authority. "You'll like her, Micileen, she's a grand wee woman."

But I feel agitated, wanting this dream to follow the usual pattern. There's a vital need to solve the immediate business problems in order to face my staff tomorrow. I'm confused. After all, if my mother has waited over sixty years surely ...

I want to wake and then go back to sleep again just to have the familiar old dream. But now, shamefully, I realize my selfishness. If my mother wishes to meet me how can I refuse?

My father takes both my hands in his and looks me straight in the eyes. "Micileen. Son." His voice has become a soft embrace and I'm no match for his charm. "Forget the worries of today. They can be solved. But, believe me, this cannot wait."

He looks down and I follow his gaze. There, lying on the ground between us, is the still body of a man. With a jolt which shakes me to the core I recognize myself. I slowly realize that this is not the old dream any more. There will be no more old dreams. What's happening is not a dream at all.

The sun has disappeared behind the hill now, but to me, everything is bathed in a golden, translucent light. Together my father and I walk up the hill, side by side, hand in hand. I'm like a child again, skipping along, up this hill for the last time. And, for the first time in sixty-two years I am going to meet my mother, who I have never known.

And I am overjoyed.

A GAME OF COWBOYS

Precisely at twelve noon, for the past five months, a tall gangling man, dressed in shabby clothes appears between the high pillars of the back gates of the warehouse where I am manager. Feet spread, fingers curled and poised, he is ready for the draw. Waiting just inside the big doorway of the stores, across the yard, ready to step out and confront him, is a tall man in a pale blue business suit. My assistant and I busy ourselves with checking lists. But out of the corner of our eyes we watch closely.

"Hey you!", the gangly man's shrill voice echoes across the yard and the man in the blue suit takes a step forward from the shadows. They reach for their "six-guns"; simultaneously blazing away "Bam! Bam! Bam!" Each time they play out this charade the man in the business suit gets plugged first and stumbles back. The gangly man always wins — because the one in the blue suit lets him.

Nothing unusual about this. Every town has its "Shoots" or its "Bang Bang" character. It might seem unusual for an old waster of a man and one in the prime of his life to play a game of cowboys almost every morning. You would think at least one of them had better things to do but, you see, and this is the difference — the man in the blue suit is our Managing Director, Frank D. Barnes and "Bam Bam", as we call the gangly one, is his father. The staff in the warehouse and the stores and the offices all know who "Bam Bam" is. The sad thing is everybody knows it except him and that is why they turn a sorry eye on this little pageant every noon. Not only is "Bam Bam" the father of our Managing Director, but, incredible as it may seem, he is also the owner of this whole complex of plumbing store, timber yard, D.I.Y. shop, tool shop and builder's providers. Strangers shake their heads incredulously when told this, and who could blame them.

Furthermore, "Bam Bam", or to give him his rightful name, James Daniel Barnes, is the chairman of the board and nobody around here would ever tolerate an unsavoury word against him.

James Daniel Barnes, known to everyone simply as J.D., in his day, was something of a tycoon. He built up this huge business from almost nothing. He started off by taking over his father's small plumbing business when he was only fifteen, when his dad died suddenly - from liver failure. Young J.D., knew almost as much as his dad about plumbing, having accompanied him on numerous working trips from an early age, even, at times, having to drive the old van. He was fond of telling us later, with a knowing wink, that earning his living was a thousand times better than being "stuck in dat auld school". And, it's obvious, too, that he enjoyed taking risks, because at the time, the place where he opened his first plumbing supplies shop was three miles from the centre of the town on a quiet country road.

Young J. D., it seemed, was never one for taking the obvious route and must have had a hunch about the future, because today, his business is surrounded by housing estates and well positioned just off the dual carriageway. J.D. Barnes was the local supplier and, with surprising speed he built up the business, expanding department by department, to what it is today. When I was at school with his sons it was already a thriving business and himself driving around in a long white Jaguar car, the first of its kind in these parts and the envy of us all.

J. D. quickly became a highly respected business man in the county. He ran for election in the Town Council and soon became a popular Councilor. But to see that man now, gaunt, in ill-fitting clothes, shuffling on his daily walk from the nursing home into town and back would break your heart as it does his son's, and ours, every day.

He is a rich man, of course, but he doesn't remember that either. He doesn't need to wear shabby clothes. But, no matter how many new suits Frank leaves for him at the nursing home, he wears them only once.

He wears it to the Thrift shop, changes into old clothes in the fitting room, pays for them, then donates the new suit to the shop. This nettled his son, as his father was always a fastidious dresser, but the Thrift shop staff, recently, have taken to simply wrapping it up and returning it to Frank who sends it back to the nursing home again.

The question in everyone's mind is, where did it all go wrong? What reduced J.D. from a wealthy and highly regarded businessman to the local bum who goes around shouting "Hey you" at everyone and blasting them with his imaginary "six-guns". It will remain a mystery until something prods his lost memory or shocks him back to his old dynamic self. I, like all who associated with him, from the senior staff to the board of directors to the women in the canteen, want this to happen soon. After all he is still the chairman of the company, his company, and we all want him back at the helm where he belongs.

It is common knowledge that J. D. got wealthy fairly quickly. He had an uncanny knack for being in the right place at the appropriate time. The complex of housing estates which now surround his yards and warehouses were the cause of the original growth of the company. He supplied every piece of plumbing to every house. And considering that he was only in his early twenties when he secured the contracts it was something of a coup. He then began to expand into building supplies and once again he was successful in supplying to the new estates growing like satellites around him. His subsequent election to the Town Council and later to the County Council came fairly quickly before he was thirty. When his sons and I were at school and going through our "skinhead" phase, it was presumed that J.D. would be the next, and youngest ever, chairman of the County Council. If his son's shaved head and safety-pin jewelry, or his friends, were ever an embarrassment to him, for we spent a lot of time in his house, it being the largest and boasting the latest TV and Hi-Fi equipment, he never complained. Later the local papers were hailing him as a surety in the next General Election to take a seat. But that was before his sudden strange trips abroad and the period he went missing.

There is only rumour and speculation about what happened to J.D. while he was ten years on the missing list. Unfortunately, we don't have his story as he has hardly spoken a full sentence to anyone since he stepped of the bus five months ago, emaciated, and collapsed in a heap at the bus station. It was as if all his remaining energy had been harnessed to get him to this point in time. It was the old ambulance driver who recognized him and rang Frank at his office. There was nobody else from the family left in town. J.D's wife, Maura, had passed away several years before and his eldest son, James Junior, after a row with his father, had emigrated to Australia as soon as he left school, and had not kept in touch.

It was after his younger son, Frank, graduated with an Economics degree and was brought into the business that J.D. suddenly started taking long trips abroad. It was assumed that he had gone in search of James Junior but now, it seems certain, this was not the case.

J.D. would come home from these trips with hardly a comment or explanation about where he had been or what he had seen, but with a restless glint in his eyes and a frenzied vigour for work. He would produce from his pockets or baggage weird souvenirs. These were mostly about the size of a fist and resembled squat females or horned bulls, or the like, with grotesque expressions painted in bizarre colours. These he lined up on the sitting-room mantelpiece against much protest from his wife, who became more troubled with each trip her husband undertook. An almost demonic look would flash from his eyes at these moments. The law was duly laid down that his collection was not to be interfered with under any circumstances. But, two years after J.D. went missing the last time, Maura, in a fit of desperation, flung the whole lot into the bin. People say that it was from this time that her health began to deteriorate and she died shortly afterwards.

It is a real mystery to everyone how J.D. managed to arrive home. Naturally, Frank had attempts made to trace his wanderings. But there is no record of his father having come through any known air or ferry port. He was not carrying a passport when he stepped of the bus. His journey out, ten years previously, stops dead in London. There was no large withdrawal from his bank account at the time and none at all in the interim. So how did he live? There is speculation that he was a government spy. This idea we find incredulous, but, who knows? And, if so, who sent him and why and where? And, above all, how did he end up in his present sorry state?

His son had forensic experts scrutinize his clothes thread by thread. There were strange seeds in the turn-up of his trousers traced to Venezuela. Hairs of animals from the forests of Borneo and female hair from a remote tribe of hill people in Mongolia were identified. Traces of arsenic and D.D.T. have been found in his system. There is a fist sized tattoo on his back behind his heart like five snakes entwined, but without heads. Photographs of this and zigzag scars on his upper arms have been distributed to anthropologists around the world, but to no avail. There is a strange phrase he is heard to mutter now and again. Frank has managed to have it recorded and sent all over the world to linguistic experts. They have shaken their heads over it. Perhaps it's just gibberish.

Visits to his home; meetings with members of the board of directors; the old parish priest; his old family doctor. Nothing had jogged J.D's memory. The Analysts in the nursing home have not ruled out the possibility that he could have been the victim of witch doctors in some remote part of the globe. Perhaps the Amazon. Maybe Central Africa - who knows! His son has left no possible test untried. But nothing has worked so far. Weird drugs in remote places, some say. Others hint at Voodoo. Nobody knows for certain. But something brought him back to his hometown and that, we are told is, in itself, positive and hopeful. And, some say, miraculous.

The doctors tell us not to give up. Not to treat him like a stranger. Not to ignore him. Don't avoid eye contact even though you get an uneasy feeling when you look into his hooded eyes. Something, somewhere, someday, will hopefully supply the jolt to bring him back from the dark edge of his mind to reality.

We pray for the day when this odd game of cowboys comes to an end. The day when the gangly man known as "Bam Bam" appears in the gateway of our yard and instead of shouting "Hey You", will call instead, "Hey, son. It's me, Dad. I'm home".

HANGING IN

"They're very interesting, of course," the Gallery proprietor said, turning away from Angela's paintings and, adjusting his bowtie, feigned interest in passers-by through the window. She studied his narrow back, her artist's eye automatically dividing the play of light and shade on the back of his shirt, while waiting for him to speak again.

She knew she had taken a chance bringing her work to this gallery. Landscapes and portraits by established artists, none of which strayed from the conventional, surrounded her. Their cozy commercialism indicated that her work was unlikely to be accepted here but she was determined to approach every gallery in the city. There must be at least one who would recognize her talent.

Angela's paintings, lined up along the bottom of the white wall, were a stark contrast to the existing exhibition above them. From her pictures the features and limbs of imaginary people, stared at the viewer, superimposed on clothes they might have worn, hung out to dry on clothes lines in a multitude of settings. They hung upside down, some dangling limply, some twisted as if in agony, others entwined like lovers; in back yards, gardens, the balconies of high rise flats and draped across bushes at the roadside camp of *Travelers*. This was the first time since graduating from art college a year ago that Angela had been able to sustain a theme in her painting and was excited by the potential. The raw edge she sought in her work was beginning to manifest itself.

The proprietor swiveled from the window. His eyes opened wide in surprise when he saw Angela and her paintings still there, as if she were expected to vanish while his back was turned. He rubbed his small hands together briskly to cover his irritation. Angela took a deep breath in anticipation of rejection. The man's eyes flicked to her rising breasts then, meeting her gaze, quickly slid past her to the door. She let her breath out slowly, suppressing her anger, remembering someone telling her once that she was much too pretty to be an artist. Stubbornly she stood her ground.

The proprietor cleared his throat. "We're booked up for quite a while," he said, his gaze now focused on some point in mid-air behind her. "In fact it would be at least ... oh, six months, before we even begin to look at new work again."

She nodded, accepting the obvious rejection in his tone, knowing it would be the same story in six months time.

As she bent to retrieve her paintings she was aware of his eyes appraising her again now that she was no longer watching. Sod him, she thought angrily, if he'd paid more attention to my paintings ... ! Shrugging off her annoyance, she stacked her work carefully into the portfolio and zipped it shut.

He walked with her to the door and, opening it to let her out, paused in the entrance to squint up at the sky as if checking for rain, although the sun shone brightly on the mid-morning street, so that Angela had to squeeze past.

"Come back in a few months time, dear," he continued, resting a hand momentarily on the small of her back. Her teeth clenched in fury at the man's effrontery. "Let's see how we're fixed by then," he concluded, swinging the door closed behind her.

I don't think so, you bastard, Angela swore under her breath as she hurried down the street..

In the past week she had shown her portfolio to five gallery owners. The reaction was much the same. 'Come back in six months.' 'You don't do landscapes by any chance?' 'Not developed enough for us, I'm afraid.' or, 'We may mount a group show early next year, perhaps then.'

Disheartening though the process was she had no intention of giving up. There were hundreds of artists ahead of her but, she reminded herself, they had had to start somewhere too.

Back at her flat Angela threw herself on the bed with relief, breathing in the familiar creamy aroma of paint and linseed oil which always had a soothing effect on her. Time, give me time and I'll hang with the best! It's just a matter of hanging in there, she reassured herself, smiling at the pun.

The screech of Tony's motorbike pulling up outside woke her from her daydreaming. Before she had time to swing her legs to the floor he had bounded up the stairs and flung himself beside her enveloping her in his arms and an aura of petrol and warm grease.

“I can see it went well for you,” he teased. “Resting after a hard morning’s bargaining with the arty-farty galleries, huh?”

“Same old story,” Angela said, snuggling closer to him. “Give them pretty landscapes. That’s all they want.”

“They’re only shopkeepers, like you say.” He kissed her ear. “They’re not ready for you yet.”

Angela pulled away from him and sat up. “What time is it, anyway? It must be lunchtime. Are you hungry?”

“Constantly,” Tony replied, pulling her back in a fierce hug, kissing her hungrily and unzipping her jeans.

After their lovemaking, Tony lay naked in the sunlight streaming through the window, blowing smoke rings towards the ceiling. Angela, wrapped in a dressing gown was brewing coffee in the small kitchen.

“Hey, listen,” he called, “why don’t you paint me? Y’know, reclining ‘Adonis’ and all that? You could pretty it up in a landscape for them.”

Angela carried the coffee into the bedroom and sat on the edge of the bed. As she handed him a mug she glanced down the length of his well defined body which he kept in shape by working out twice weekly in the gym

"No," she sighed, “too small. That’s the problem."

"Too small ... ?” he snorted. "That’s now, after the deed is done. But not before, remember?”

Angela laughed and slapped his muscled thigh playfully. "No, I don’t mean that, you eejit. It's my work I'm talking about." She stretched out her arms, slopping coffee onto the bed, causing him to jump back. "Bigger canvasses," she explained.

Tony flexed his muscles and winked at her. "Think big, that's what I always say." And, swinging himself off the bed, downed his coffee and zipped himself back into his clothes. "Gotta get back to the garage," he said, kissing her goodbye.

As the bike roared into the distance Angela was seized with sudden inspiration. Whisking the white linen sheets off her bed, oblivious to the fact they were a recent and expensive gift from her mother, Angela tugged until they ripped down the centre. Satisfied, she dropped them on the floor and raced outside to the garden shed where she remembered seeing a few lengths of timber and some rusting tools.

It was hard going with the old rusty saw but she managed to hack through them. She hammered the laths together into rough frames then stretched the sheets tightly over them. Working quickly she primed them, throwing the windows wide open to let out the pungent smell, then stood back viewing her work with satisfaction. Four large canvasses stood against the wall.

A bit rough, she thought, but they'll do for now. I must find a studio, this bedroom is too cramped. Maybe that's why I work so small. I need more space.

While waiting for the primer to dry Angela wondered how she could get her hands on some big brushes. Then she remembered seeing several old household paintbrushes at her mother's. Without pausing to put on a jacket she raced out the door. Along the canal a woman and child threw crusts to the ducks. Angela watched as diamonds of light scattered along the gentle ripples. Pretty pictures, she thought ironically.

A sudden outburst of squabbling and squawking pierced the air as a flock of seagulls swooped out of the blue sky, dive-bombing the crusts and trying to scatter the ducks. On their home territory, and bigger than their scavenging sea cousins, the ducks chased them off, running along the top of the water screeching and spreading their wings in anger. The gulls soared and wheeled in preparation for another attack.

Angela watched the flying battle in amazement. The gulls don't usually come this far inland, she thought, unless a storm is brewing. She checked the sky behind her and could almost feel the weight of the large electric-grey cloud, pregnant with rain, blowing over the rooftops from the sea.

It was one of those summer squalls that springs unexpectedly out of the Atlantic. The excitement of the battle in the water below and the approaching storm above thrilled her. For a moment she stood, transfixed against the canal railings, filled with a fusion of the beauty, power and violence of nature.

This, she realized, was the missing element in her paintings. The instilled passion of life. A storm didn't ask for permission to blow; it raged regardless, sweeping all in its path. Seagulls swooped unceremoniously; aware only of the dictations of hunger. Tony didn't seek approval to make love to her; he took his pleasure brazenly. But the final thought made her wince. Perhaps she should be more stringent with him. Perhaps he was beginning to take her for granted. She put the thought to the back of her mind deciding to think about it later.

As she watched the scene before her, Angela recalled her early childish drawings hidden in the back of her copybooks. The pleasant little paintings to please her father. Praise for neat, careful work from teachers. Never really letting herself go. All through life, all through art college, Angela saw now, how she had tried to please everyone except herself. Talent was not lacking, she knew, but somehow the fiery passion rumbling deep inside her had always been doused by a desire to please others. Even her brushes were small, her drawing boards manageable, as if she had a fear of what she might do if that passion was given its head. It did not hinder her graduating with a distinction. But that was college, she mused, out here is real life.

The rain, suddenly unleashed, pelted the canal water like pellets. Seagulls wheeled. Ducks thrashed. Mother grabbed her screeching child and ran for the shelter of the trees. Only Angela danced with joy as the wind squalled and rain soaked her.

"Yes!" she whooped triumphantly, "tearing those sheets was an inspiration!" It was as if ripping them was an act preempting the storm, renting the sky, with its unbridled force.

When she arrived at her mother's house her clothes were saturated.

"Holy God, Angela," her mother scolded, when she saw her standing inside the kitchen door, a pool of water gathering at her feet. "Have you no raincoat? Quick child, run up to my room and change into something dry before you catch your death ..." Her mother, a smaller, plumper version of her daughter, draped in a flowery apron over baggy slacks, ushered her up the stairs.

It was she who had recognized Angela's need to express her talent and argued in her favour, against her husband's reluctance, to send his daughter to art college. Fortunately Angela won a scholarship so that he could not harangue her about throwing his money away on, what he called, a wasted life. He would have preferred to see her use her aptitude in maths to follow him in his profession of accountancy. Unfortunately he did not live to see her graduate four years later.

"Mam," Angela said as she traipsed downstairs and bundled her wet clothes into the dryer. "I need to get some things from the garage."

Her mother gazed at her in amusement. Dressed in one of her old cotton dresses, her daughter looked more like a younger sister.

"It's a long time since I was able to squeeze into that," she remarked, laughing. "But what things do you want from the garage. I can't remember when I was last out there. You'd better ask Francis when he gets home. It's his domain now." Francis was Angela's younger brother and training in furniture design.

"Oh, just saws and hammers and ..." Angela thought for a moment. "Have we still got the large paintbrushes ?

Her mother shrugged. "I suppose so. Francis would know. But wait, I'm sure some of the old things are still in a box under the stairs. I don't think he'd like you taking his things."

"Thanks," Angela said and went out to the hallway to rummage in the cupboard under the stairs. "They're here all right," she called and dragged the box into the kitchen. She selected what she wanted then said without looking up. "Mam. I'm thinking of leaving."

“Leaving?” Her mother turned from the sink and stared at her. "The flat?"

"No." Angela took a deep breath before continuing. "Town. Maybe go abroad."

“When ... Why? But I thought you were happy here?”

Angela shifted uneasily seeing how this sudden announcement had shocked her mother. It had taken her by surprise too, the words were out of her mouth before she realized what she had said herself. “I need to get out. Find a proper place to work. Y’know, this place is too small.”

Her mother laughed disconcertedly. “Well,” she began, then stopped, not knowing what to say next.

“Not right away,” Angela hurried on, backpedaling now, to take some of the sting out of her decision. For herself as well as her mother. “I need more space to work. I need to ... Oh I don’t know. Travel a bit ... See more ...”

The ideas came tumbling out of their own accord and, as they did, taking Angela more and more by surprise, the excitement of getting away and seeing the world stimulated her. It was as if the decisions were out of her hands now. As if some other authority had taken over.

"And what about Tony," her mother started in alarm. "What will he think. He seems such a nice lad. I thought ..." She let the words trail off.

"Well, maybe I'm getting too attached. Oh, I dunno ... It's ... " Angela shook her head and hurried on as if to shake away any guilt feelings before they took root. "Y'know. I need time ... space ... to develop. See the rest of the world. There was no chance when I was at college. And then Dad ..." She stopped abruptly. She did not want to drag his reluctance to pay for foreign travel into the conversation. And then his sudden illness ... She could see her mother's mounting anguish at these old wounds being resurrected."

The older woman slumped against the sink, entwine her hands heedlessly in her apron watching the growing excitement on her daughter's face as she elaborated her plans. She shook her head in bewilderment. Going to collage was one thing but she could see no reason to traipse around the world. That, to her, who never had any desire to be anywhere else but where she was, was only looking for trouble. She put on a brave smile. "If that's what you want dear," was all she could say.

Angela rushed to her and hugged her "I knew you'd understand," she cried.

Tears welled up in her mother's eyes. "I'm sure I don't," she said, sniffing and dabbing at her eyes with the edge of her apron. "But you seem to know what you're doing."

"It'll only be for a while," Angela said, trying to soften the blow.

"And what about money? How will you live.?"

"Odd jobs, I suppose. Everyone does it." This had been the main problem during college holidays. Her parents had refused to finance or allow her to go off with other students to work part-time in Europe. Angela could never fathom their reluctance to do so. Then, when her father had become ill, there was no point in arguing. She had had to make do with local Summer jobs. The exciting stories brought back by her friends, of foreign cities and galleries, had almost brought her to tears. She was surprised that her mother had given in so easily this time. But how could she object. I'm old enough to make my own decisions now, Angela thought. Or perhaps the suddenness of the decision and my excitement has caught her off guard.

She watched her mother dab at her eyes and turn away to fill the kettle. A cup of tea seems to be her way of concluding any disagreement. Over the sound of splashing water her mother said, "I can manage a few hundred pounds."

"No, please. I'll manage."

"You'll need it," her mother said flatly and Angela, overcome with gratitude at this sudden change of attitude hugged her again tightly. "Thanks Mam. I love you."

Later, poised with a four inch paint brush in her hand and pots of paint ready on the floor, Angela stood before the four blank canvasses in deep silence, waiting for the rush of inspiration. Waiting for the creative dam to burst and overflow, she was unaware of Tony entering the flat until his hand rested on her shoulder, making her jump.

“Swimming,” he said, grinning and waving his togs and towel in front of her face.

“Oh.” Angela jumped. “You gave me a fright.”

Tony pointed to the four canvasses. “What’s this?” he asked. “The Opus Magnus. Big, huh!” Then he noticed the bare mattress. "Jesus," he exclaimed. "What happened the sheets?"

Angela pointed distractedly at the stretched frames.

"You're mad, Angie babe!." He shook his head vigorously. "Anyway, get your togs. The tide’s in.” He checked his watch. “In ... four minutes. Let’s go.”

“I can’t.” Angela bit her lip.

Tony grinned and eased the paintbrush out of her hand. “The sun is shining,” he sang. “The tide is full. It waits for no man, or woman.”

Angela reached for the brush but Tony held it behind his back. “Come on.” He danced away from her. “This will keep. The tide won’t. I need a swim.”

Angela shook her head. “I have to work.”

“Sure,” Tony said. “But later. I’m bursting to get into the water. I need to get the grease out of my system. I’ve had a tough day. Hot as hell.”

Angela glared at him. "And I've had it cushy ...?"

“Angie. Angie,” Tony pleaded, coming and putting his arms around her.

“No, Tony. Don’t.” She pushed him away gently.

“What?” Tony looked at her, bewildered.

“I don’t mean that.” Angela said. “I have to do this,” She indicated the canvasses.

“Yes,” he said. “I know. But let's go swimming first. Okay.”

Angela frowned in anguish. How could she refuse to go swimming? But she had to start painting. It was important. “I have to do this,” she said adamantly.

“Angie?”

“Look, you go on ahead,” she said, forcing a smile. "I can ..."

But Tony did not wait for her to finish. He dangled the paintbrush between his thumb and forefinger, before her face, then dropped it at her feet. Turning abruptly, he stomped from the room without a word.

“Tony.” Angela took a step after him. “Tony ...!”

The only reply she got was the street door banging shut behind him and the roar of his motorbike engine snarling down the street.

“Oh, damn,” Angela cried. She picked up the paintbrush and turned to the canvasses and glared at them.

“You,” she hissed angrily between clenched teeth. Then, filling her brush with paint, she flung it with all her energy at the first canvas.

It struck and splattered like an exploding firecracker, before sliding down the surface, leaving a thick stream of deep vermilion in its wake. Angela stared at it through hot tears welling up and stinging her eyes in frustration. She wiped them away with the back of her hand. The deep gash of red, cutting the white ground like an open wound, danced before her. She stooped and picked up the paintbrush once more and filled it. As she began to spread the paint, elaborating on the gash, opening it out as if searching for a definition, her anger slowly dissipated, leaving a void which gradually filled with excitement.

Time evaporated. Swabs of colour in thick impasto gathered force, producing shapes that boiled up inside her, taking her unawares, merging and molding together in swirling abstract mass. Weighty purple storm clouds fought for space with pink streaked flocks of birds. Hovering menacingly, motorbikes roared through electric skies, underscored by bejeweled rippling waters. Working feverishly, brain and limbs stretched to their limits, Angela was drawn out of herself and transported, mesmerized by the shapes and colours emerging before her.

Finally, every ounce of energy drained from her, she dropped her brushes and fell exhausted on the sheet-stripped bed. The four large canvasses stood against the walls, transformed and triumphant, as she herself was by the power of latent forces which had taken her over and, it seemed, sucked the very substance from her soul.

The voice inside her trumpeted, "I am an artist. And I must be free!"

Exultant, throwing wide her arms as if to embrace the ceiling - the walls - the street, the feeling inside her swelled until she could almost feel herself enfold the whole world.

CURVE IN FRAME

Eugene was last in line at the pastry counter, and as the assistant turned to serve him, the curve of her hip was so graceful, he sucked in his breath as the beauty of it struck him. Is it this easy to fall in love? he wondered.

For Stella, his girlfriend, and himself it had not been love-at-first-sight. They had met two years previously after their respective lovers had jilted them, meeting through various groups of acquaintances for a number of weeks before they had finally taken serious notice of each other.

"I'd say we got each other on the rebound," Stella had remarked stoically when it finally happened.

"Rebound or not, 'I'll drink to that'," he replied happily, delighted once again, at the age of thirty six, to be on the brink of a new relationship.

Now standing at the shop counter on this dismal Monday morning, so many minutes past the hour, when he should have been at his desk, Eugene savored the moment. You're looking at me, looking at you, looking at me, and we're both relishing it.

It was only an hour ago, he remembered with a jolt, that he had left Stella's warm embrace. A mere eighty six thousand four hundred film frames ago their moist lover's bodies had parted, allowing the cool air of morning to ripple between them.

It had not been the warmest of partings on this dull October morning. Her flat was drafty, especially when the wind huffed in from the East. Eugene was well used to that but their chilly parting baffled him. Their love-making this morning had not been as perfect as usual, although it was only point-one off. Only he, it seemed, had been aware of it. The coldness, whether real or imagined, was in the emotional rather than the physical sense, he decided, and certainly did not come from him. Was it because Stella was flying off on a field-trip with her professor this very morning? As far as he was concerned the relationship was all it should be. Loving. Agreeable. Fun. Steady. Stella was the best and he loved her.

The assistant broke in on his thoughts asking him what he would like.

"Eh ... um," his tongue stumbling over the words, "six ... um, doughnuts, please. Thanks."

He watched her pick up the tongs and reach with a flourish into the display cabinet. The ballet-like movement of her arm resembled the effortless flight of a long necked bird. Eugene was enthralled. He wanted to see her turn again and quickly pointed to the chocolate covered doughnuts on the shelf behind her.

"No, sorry, I ... um ... meant those ones."

The girl swiveled without breaking her rhythm and once again Eugene marveled at her grace. His mind clocked in the moment. It was the twenty-first-minute-after-nine, on the fourteenth day of the tenth month. A drizzly Monday morning. A moment he would store away to ponder and decipher at leisure over a pint with his friend Patrick, who envied the ease with which he fell in love. All it took was, the swell of a thigh, the grace of a long neck, the trail of an eyebrow.

Eugene did not consider himself to be handsome. Long years hunched over graphic designs had given him a round shouldered stoop and a crinkled forehead. In the last five years or so he had begun to loose his hair. But sometimes when he caught himself at a certain angle in the mirror with the sun slanting across his face, he could still glimpse the boyish looks of twenty years ago. It baffled him how Stella retained the fresh bloom of a much younger woman as she spent most of her time out-doors. In looks there was a gap of ten years between them. In reality only one.

The shop assistant's laugh drew his attention to a group of women giggling and joking at the back of the shop. Being so pre-occupied in his fantasy, he had not heard them come in. Turning to look he listened for a moment as they ribbed each other about their men, cracking jokes off each other loud enough for anyone to hear, enjoying their own buffoonery. Eugene turned back and joined in the girl's laughter. The throbbing of her throat as she did so intoxicated him.

He thought about how Patrick would playfully chide him later. "Aren't you the right romantic," he could almost hear his friend say. "It's not a modern day graphic artist at all you should be, but apprenticed to an Old Master. The trouble with you is, you succumb all too easily to a strong sensuous line."

But now, as Eugene watched the girl popping doughnuts into a bag with the refinement of a society hostess, his belief in love-at-first-sight was bolstered and a warm glow surged through his veins.

What am I going to do about it, he wondered, that's the next question. And Patrick would be sure to ask.

For the moment he pushed 'the next question' to the back of his mind. It was something to be recalled and mulled over, like a still from a movie; the exact frame studied over and over again, regardless of whether he did or did not do anything about it right now.

At this precise moment the scene was recording itself on the emulsion of his mind. In this instant he registered the girl's lustrous eyes, the fluid movements of her body, and the accentuated swivel of her hips just visible across the top of the low counter displaying body-language both innocent and alluring, as she curved in the frame of his eye. At the same time Eugene felt his own body-language answering in response. Exhilarated, he credited himself with having set the entire scene in motion.

Patrick would tease him on that too. He could hear him laughing already. "You always have to be the instigator," his friend would say before breaking into an off-key parody of his favorite song, "Oh, Ho, Oh, Yes I'm The Great Ins-tig-a-tor ...," while poking him in the shoulder in time to the tune.

Eugene decided he would not discuss it with Patrick at all. He was too cynical for his boots. His pseudo-scientific reasoning would break it down and offer elaborate explanations, spoiling the fun.

The assistant broke in on his reverie. "Will that be all?" she asked, her voice a lilting song to his ears, as she handed him the bag of doughnuts.

Eugene racked his brain for something to say to stall the moment of leaving. Just to hear that voice again. *Are you new here? Where's the usual girl? I haven't seen you here before?*

She was still smiling at him and holding out the bag. He did not take it straight away. He told himself it was more than just a smile. It was an invitation. A signal to him to get to know her better.

Hold it! he warned himself, hold it right there, you are in love with Stella. She loves you. You have been together for two years. It's a wonderful relationship. Do you want to spoil it? Calm down. Take your doughnuts. Go to work.

A hundred options fast-forwarded through the camera of his brain. *Invite her for a coffee. Ask her to lunch. Make a date for after work.* Stella would be gone for over a week. Could he have a brief encounter for a few days in her absence? Tell the woman it would only last a week. Come clean with her*! Did she have a man? Would it matter?* She *was* flirting with him *wasn't* she? He was excited. How he would love to run his hand over that curving hip. To feel her fingers gripping the muscles of his back. Now she was laughing, and her laugh was tinkling crystals on his ears. Then, she made a movement with her free hand, and it seemed to Eugene as if she had reached through the counter and caressed his thigh with her warm palm. His fingers touched the spot in wonder. He felt himself getting hot, his mind balmy and excited.

If he tried to explain that, Patrick would laugh, a huge guffaw, and talk about telekinesis ... And who was she? Which shop? Suddenly Patrick would pretend to have a great longing for doughnuts. He would go first thing the next morning. He was looking for a woman just like that ...!

Or he might chide him. "Ach, sure, man, it was all in your much-too-fertile imagination. You temperamental artists! Stella had upset your little apple barrel by not giving you the full treatment this morning, and you willed the rest - oh, not consciously of course - but willed it all the same. You had to dominate something. Stella - okay, for once - didn't allow you to dominate her.

So you, just one jump ahead of our friend the ape, still needed to dominate something to appease your male ego. You made it happen. Set the whole thing in motion. Now, me boy, if you could only control that. Now wouldn't that be something ...!"

Since the first time two years ago, when Eugene and Stella had first loved each other, it was as if their bodies, minds, moods, needs and desires were as one. But this morning it had only been ninety-nine-point-nine per cent. That one single frame, the point-one per cent, had stuck in Eugene's mind. It should have burnt up and disintegrated before his eyes as a frame in a real film would when it sticks in the projector's glaring light. But it didn't.

Was it because Stella was flying off to work in the sunny Mediterranean on this grey October morning?

Well, yes of course, that was part of it. But it did not fully explain his dilemma. There was something else. Stella had tried to explain to him, but he did not fully understand. Too scientific for him. He wasn't interested in marine biology. They had never taken a great interest in each others jobs. In this aspect, they were miles apart, although they appreciated, respected, and loved each other, anything they did, outside of other love affairs, was their own business.

But in the pub last night with Stella's colleagues Eugene felt completely out of his depth and she hadn't thrown him any life-lines. And then there was her boss, the Professor, whom Eugene had never met before, who wasn't much older than himself, and who lavished more attention on Stella than a boss should ... So it seemed to Eugene.

Brooding on this at the counter, when the shop assistant turned from the customer ahead of him, Eugene was so struck by the voluptuous curve of her hip and her blazing smile, that his mind screamed recklessly; *Oh you're so beautiful!* It startled him so much, for a moment he panicked, thinking he had shrieked out loud.

If he ever described the moment to Patrick he would be careful to play it down. "Oh, it was just one of those magical moments," or perhaps, "y'know, love in the instant," or maybe, "just one of those things,"?

Then, his friend would coax him to recall it frame by frame, his small black eyes blinking rapidly as all the little details that made the moment flicker and come to life were filled in, running slowly through the projector of their minds. And Patrick breaking it down with pretentious and indecipherable explanations.

Never! Edit now. Keep your mouth shut. Don't breath a word to your boozing friend. And none will be the wiser. Unlike the time when I first admitted my love for Stella, he recalled. Before I had even told her.

He remembered the night clearly. He and Patrick were standing at the bar when Stella entered. Before he had time to stop him, Patrick had thrown an arm about both their shoulders and scooped them like a mother hen under the great black wings of his overcoat. "Ah. Love," he intoned, wiping imaginary tears of emotion from his cheeks and almost crushing their heads in the process, "The converging lines of our lives meeting at the horizon of expectancy."

"Yes. But only on paper," Eugene began, struggling in Patrick's firm grasp to extract a pen from his inside pocket to demonstrate. "In reality, as every schoolboy knows, they only appear to meet ..."

"Appearances are merely deceptions," Patrick huffed, chocking him off.

Stella smiled encouragingly across at Eugene from under their friends arm. "Yes. . ."

"Absolutely!" Patrick pronounced, giving them a final bone crushing hug before releasing them.

"Anyway," Stella explained. "I'm a ship ..."

"Of course you are," Patrick reiterated. "And a fine ship indeed if I might say so. And god bless all who sail in ..."

"Not a train." Stella cut him off, laughing.

"Train ...?" Eugene was beginning to loose the thread of the conversation. But he didn't care. He was more fascinated by Stella's soft doe-like eyes which were gazing auspiciously at him across

Patrick's beer-belly. He couldn't take his eyes off her. Although secretly wishing he had not told Patrick about his feelings for her, at the same time he was delighted that his friend had assumed Stella knew and taken the initiative.

"Nothing so gross!" Patrick continued.

Eugene wanted to talk about more important things. He sidled around Patrick and wedged himself beside Stella. Her eyes sparkled at him.

Patrick glowered, "Converging train tracks indeed," he sneered, "this lady cares not for tracks, converging or not. The lady is a ship. A starry ship that sails on celestial seas ..."

"Sink or swim." Stella cut him short. "That's me." She gave Eugene a charming girlish smile.

Eugene grinned back at her, ignoring Patrick. But Patrick would crow later, that it was he who had finally brought them together.

Stella asked him. "Do you swim?"

"Like a stone," he joked.

"Seriously ..?" she asked eagerly.

Eugene was lost in the deep pool of her eyes. Recognizing that Stella was opening herself to his longing for her, he straightened his shoulders, pulled himself to his full height and reached for her hand. Patrick was soon forgotten as they made a date for the swimming pool.

They fell in love in the water, their eyes meeting across the small ripples in the pool. And then they were aching to touch, but at first only by accident, swimming close together and brushing against each other. They were both adequate swimmers. Six lengths apiece. Both over-arm and breast-stroke.

After the swim, over a beer, they talked ardently about themselves. A few hours later they were both in their separate beds, restless, wishing already for the next encounter. But Stella had gone away on a field-trip soon after and Eugene had been swamped with work. They met spasmodically after that and it was not until a few months later that they finally came together as lovers.

Guilt crept up and tapped Eugene on the shoulder. How could he do this to Stella? Stand here lusting after this woman with the doughnuts ... No. This had to stop.

Edit now, his heart cried, before it's too late. Cut the last reel. Pretend it never happened.

Ah, but it did, his conscience scoffed. As Eugene knew well, every editor knows what he has discarded. And any editor worth his scissors could create a new scenario from the bits on the cutting room floor. And with a twist of imagination make it - he dared not think - incriminating.

His mind fast-forwarded to Stella's return, enthusiastic and suntanned, a week from now.

"And what did you do while I was away?" she would enquire.

"Oh, nothing much. The usual. Work."

"Miss me. Huh?"

"Of course."

"You didn't get up to anything wild ... Nothing I wouldn't do?"

"Wild? It rained all the time."

"Oh. That's awful. Really awful."

"Bought some chocolate doughnuts."

"Doughnuts ...?"

Panic-stricken, Eugene envisages the floor strewn with the cuttings of the illicit film. Careful, he warns himself. Quick, change the subject. Play cool. Notice her suntan. Anything but doughnuts! Take her in your arms. It's been a whole week ...

"Com'ere you sexy suntanned ... Hmmmmmm!"

Lost in reverie he stands clutching the bag of buns.

The shop assistant's voice brought him back to reality. "That'll be three-sixty, please."

“What ... Oh ... Of course.”

Already she had passed her smile on to the customer behind him. Depleted, Eugene fumbled in his pocket for the money and handed it to the girl.

As she turned to the cash register he closed his eyes. He couldn’t trust himself to look. With the bag of doughnuts in one hand and his change in the other, Eugene headed into the street. The drizzle had given way to a thick, depressing fog, enveloping everything as far as the eye could see.

With a jerk he remembered his fellow workers waiting for him to bring back the doughnuts for their coffee break.

Pulling up his collar against the cold mist, he stuffed the change in his pocket and hurried to the studio, feeling guilty at his fantasies, wondering if Stella's flight had taken off after all?

PIRATE PETE

We called him Pirate Pete. He limped and had a black patch over one eye. His clothes were shapeless and soiled, all black, except for a red handkerchief at his throat. That and his weathered skin gave him a Gypsy-like appearance. He also sailed a small fishing boat. We fantasized that he was a Gypsy of the sea, even though we had ever seen a real Gypsy, except in books. How did he acquire the name? He was older that any of our fathers and rarely discussed. Particularly in our house, where inquisitiveness about other people was not encouraged.

We met him almost every day on our way back to school. He was caretaker of the local 'flea-pit'; the Star cinema. A dark and sticky place, where, it was rumoured a woman once slipped out of her tight shoes to ease her feet and when she went to slip them back there was a mouse in one of them.

One of my friends fathers said Pete once owned the Star cinema. We imagined it was only a rumour.

He'd lean over the little bridge, a short-cut to both school and cinema, invariably chewing a wad of tobacco. We delighted in shouting, *'Pirate Pete has no sheet, sleeps out in the rain and sleet,'* made up in anticipation of getting a chase. But of course he never rose to the taunt. He responded, turning slowly, his huge jaws working on the cud of tobacco, glaring at us with his good eye. Was it my imagination, I wondered, that he seemed to single me out when he spat a big gob of tobacco juice in our direction?

One of our great pastimes at break time was acting out what it would be like to be splattered by Pete's tobacco juice. One of my pals, a natural comic, kept us in stitches pretending to be hit by one of Pete's 'cannon-balls'. Acting out taking the full whack of the load, and Pete chewing and spitting as well.

It was hilarious in day-light but I had nightmares of Pete spitting and catching me, waking up, terrified, just in time, before being pulverized with his huge fists.

We schoolboy friends grew up and eventually went our own ways. News of Pirate Pete's death came from a chance meeting with one of the lads in Dublin. He said it was a small funeral. We drank a pint to his memory and for half an hour Pirate Pete relived in our memories.

Later, on one of my rare visits home, I was in the local pub waiting for the lads. The man sitting next to me supped his pint and passed some small talk. I was only giving him half my attention. He rambled on regardless until I heard the words Star Cinema. I began to take more notice.

He recalled all the old pictures he had seen there as a young lad - most of which were unknown to me. He must have been older than he looked if he remembered these films, because I recognized names from the silent era. Then, to my surprise, he asked me. “I don’t suppose you’d remember The Pirate?”

“Of course I do”. I told him.

“Buried him three months ago. God rest his soul.”

I nodded in sympathy. My companion took out an old pipe and struck a match to it. “Aye, we buried him, eye-patch and all.” He pulled on the pipe before continuing. "Changed his whole life, the eye did. Used to be a fine hardy man. All the girls were crazy after him, 'til the eye."

I tried to picture Pete as a young dashing Valentino, but couldn't.

"Never forgave the young wastrel who gave it to him, or his kin...”

The man took a long swig from his pint and raised his glass to signal for another. I did likewise and insisted. "My treat." My companion gave me a nod. "Decent man." Then he continued. “Jeremiah Corcoran, that was his real name y'know. Once owned the old ‘flea-pit’, he did. He brung pictures to this town before pictures were ever heard off. Oh aye, he was a celebrity then. Used to ride one of them big motor bikes with twenty one gears. What was it called… a Guzzi something… Oh, he was the right divil in them days..."

The man puffed on his pipe for a minute, watching his new pint settling.

“By Gobs, the young fillies were mad about him then. Used to go up on the big bike with him jizzing all over the place. He was never without a good-looker hangin' onto him. Could've had any one of them. But the eye business finished him. Wouldn't get up on the old bike after that and took to the drink. Poured the entire 'flea-pit’ down his throat. Lost it, lock, stock and barrel. No self-repectin' young one would even look at him after that.

I was intrigued and ashamed at the same time. How we kids had jeered old Pete. A once proud and enterprising giant of a man, egged on for a chase, by a gang of excitable school kids.

"D’ya know he was as strong as a stallion to the end. Must’ve been over a hundred. He could’ve snapped a young sapling in his hand like that..."

While the story teller held up his own huge hand and demonstrated, I imagined how lucky we were as kids, that Pete had never caught any of us in his huge tree-snapping hands.

"...and fast on his feet, though you'd never think it..." the man continued. I shivered, thinking, I had dreamed correctly. Pirate Pete could have caught me if he wanted to. I took a long swig of my pint, now knowing how close I had come to being crushed by this formidable man.

"... but y'know somethin’? He wouldn’t’ve hurt a flea even in his own ‘pit’. The eye was the end of him. Lost him everything. His picture house, his grand big bike, his house, and his sweetheart. "Like I said, he could’ve married any one of them.” The man shook his head gravely.

I was fascinated now and eager to know more, Pete was rarely talked about in my time. By then, it seemed, he had been relegated to the low position of being just another town drunk.

"Did you know him well?" I prompted.

The man took a long swallow, drained his pint and called for another, indicating my glass as well, as he turned a watery eye on me.

"I did, an' I didn't..." He began noncommittally. "He was a distant relation o' mine, a grand-uncle on the mother's side. He used to let us into the Pictures for free. And just as well, sure we didn't have two brass ha'pennies to rub together in our pocket." He grinned in reflection, then laughed. "If we even had a pocket."

By know I was hoping none of the lads would come in until the auld codger finished his story, because I hadn't yet found out how Jeremiah Corcoran, alias Pirate Pete, had lost the eye. Up to now it seemed to me that that knowledge was lost for ever. But now my companion had turned away from me, eying the bar man pulling his pint. But I couldn't let him stop now.

"So..." I ventured, suppressing the excitement in my voice, "how did he lose it... the eye..." But he continued to ignore me until the new pints were in front of us.

"How did he lose it?" He turned and glared at me. "Sure wasn't it gouged out of his head with a penknife".

The vehemence of his words shook me.

"Every week Jeremiah hung a big wooden billboard at the bridge, with the names of the pictures for the next week. And every week the school boys would cut down the sign and throw it into the river for devilment. One day he caught them at it. He was raving mad. He rushed at them to scatter them. The one holding the knife to cut the string, panicked, lashed out, and gouged the eye out of him. A little snot of a guttersnipe if ever there was one."

I was incredulous, imagining something greater, a child's fantasy, like a battle with smugglers or a bar-room brawl, on some remote South Seas island. At least, he could have had a mighty crash on his old motorbike trying to do a ton-up. But no. A 'little snot of a guttersnipe' with a pocket knife, cutting down signs for fun to float on the river.

My story teller jammed the pipe into his mouth and turned to stare me straight in the face. "Aye. That's how it was. Stuck the knife in and pulled out the eye. Coulda killed him stone dead if it hadda gone in more. Old Jeremiah never forgave him - or his kin. But he was a gentleman. He never let it be spoken of outside the family. But it can be said now that he’s gone. The young scoundrel..." And he said the name slowly and distinctly. "It was Jimmy Joe Walsh..."

My pint froze in mid air half way to my mouth

Jimmy Joe Walsh was my father.

FADE OUT

He threw another log on the fire before slumping back, with the weight of his fifty-odd years, onto the battered couch. Here, relaxed in favorite surroundings, he looked nothing like a famous rock star but, rather, like any other man of middle years.

I sat facing him, a mite less intimidated than I'd imagined I would be, in the presence of a legend. Once again I released the pause button of my tape machine and glanced down at the list of questions scribbled in the open notebook in my lap that were there purely to prompt. I preferred for him to lead the conversation. Interviews worked better for me that way.

"Now," he drawled in that famous mid-atlantic accent, "Where were we ?" Long legs stretched towards the blaze and a lazy hand floated towards the guitar leaning against the wall. This venerable instrument was a very familiar veteran of a thousand concerts around the world. His finger plucked a string and even that single sound summoned traces of his personal magic.

He grinned at the look on my face. "Yes ... the famous Fade-Out." We listened silently to the note now dissolving softly into the shadows of the room. Something about it suddenly animated him and he sat up, looking around, as excitement lit his face.

"This room," he exclaimed, long arms gesturing wildly, "This room is my youth. Everything in it comes from the early days ... the 'good ole' days'." He laughed quietly before slumping back again as if the very memories of it tired him.

This man, I decided, was very different, here, to the one who strutted and sang in his distinctive raucous voice to millions every year. Seeing him in close-up it seemed as if life, rock 'n' roll, and all it represented, had taken its toll. He'd already told me about the traveling, week-long parties, groupies, drugs, drink, isolation, bodyguards, the media, and all the paraphernalia of international fame. It was a story that could be told of a hundred other entertainers. I wanted more.

I considered the difference between this person as opposed to the famous ‘god of rock’. He looked no different, sitting here, to any of his own denim-clad, middle-aged, male fans. How had I expected to find him in his own living room? The glittering stage personality who had out-rocked Presley and the Beatles and everyone else and led the Rock 'n' Roll world for the past thirty years. But even here, in this ordinary-looking room, the *Man* was still a god to me. More god than any of the Greek mythical variety roaming the pages of myths and legends. Here was a deity you could touch ... once you got through his agent, manager, press officer, bodyguards, friends and the massive gates of his estate. I even had to get past his cats, one of which now leapt into his lap as he sunk once more into the deep cushions of the couch.

I waited but he seemed to have forgotten me as he sat there deep in thought. The old black Persian tomcat blinked once before fixing a stare at me. I felt it was a subtle warning not to disturb the master in his reverie. Relax, the creature willed me, chill out. No hurry. It was all right for the pair of them. I had a deadline early in the morning and an uncomfortable image hovered of the editor snorting in anger when he saw an empty space with my name all over it. I'd have to stay up and write through the small hours. But it was worth it for my biggest interview coup to date. The one to make my name.

How I came by the opportunity in the first place was another, very long, story already stored on disk where it would be safe until I was ready to write the book. A definitive work on the *Man* that would stop them all in their tracks. The story of a young journalist who had wangled for five years to sit in the inner sanctum of the greatest living rock legend of the century.

I glanced at the recorder. Would there be enough tape? I hoped so.

He stirred and sat up. So too did the cat although it remained on the famous lap. How many people, I wondered, would give as many eye teeth to swap places with that old rag-bag! How many more would give a lifetime's record collection to be here in my place with the *Man* ?

"Yep, this room..." he began, then lapsed into silence again as he shooed the cat off his lap and reached for the guitar. He hugged it affectionately across his knees and strummed a chord. DRAAANNNG! The *Chord*. The famous chord that had first made the teenage world jump up and down almost thirty years ago and still held them in it's power. It cut through the subdued atmosphere like a razor blade.

It was the opening chord of his first hit single, 'Rock a Steady'. A sound that started an industry still churning and earning three decades on. Band, crew, studio, record company, record store staff, and merchandisers. Whole generations kept in employment by one man having struck that one electrifying chord all those years ago. Not just a guitar chord – but a sound that seemed to have stirred the psyche of a young generation resonating with their dreams and hopes. And me too, here now, earning my daily bread writing about him. Nobody could deny him his riches.

The opening lines ran through my head as he continued to play the melody - Rock a Steady, Rock a Steady / Rock a Through the Night / Keep a Rockin', Keep a Steady/ Alright, alright, alright! Silly words that made little sense now... but back then... And he had been rocking steadily ever since.

As a toddler I stumbled and wobbled in the kitchen with my mother as we danced to it together. Years later I came across a scratched single in a jumble sale and I bought it for her as a much appreciated Christmas present.

But the *Man* had finished strumming and was talking again. "This room's a fake." He grinned waving his long arms about. "Or should I say, an expensive designer's replica, of where I wrote that song. It was a small tatty gaff. The kind you only lived in if you had to - and we had to, back then. But you know all that. When I bought this place I had the room reproduced. It was a great joke at first. Describing it to the designer bloke, the couch, the table, the fireplace, everything. But not the curtains. Nobody, but nobody, could live with those godawful curtains.!" He laughed a deep raucous laugh. "And the wallpaper. He couldn't find the original so we had it hand-painted." He mimed a paint brush in the air.

“Yessiree. Hand - Painted. It cost a packet but ... what the hell!"

I made a quick note to find out more about the artist. He or she would be worth checking out - but not right now. Nothing must be allowed to interrupt the present proceedings.

"But, when it was finished, I knew we had created a magic room. The room where the first hit was written. Bigger, of course, and more subdued lighting, but the closest to that lucky space where I'd written that first one ... well, not exactly ... "

The *Man* broke off abruptly. I waited as the silence became weighty. Eventually he shrugged and continued. "That old *Gibson* there, "he said quietly, pointing to the guitar, "It's not even marked. It's one of the early ones he didn't bother to put his name on. Man, what an axe! I've had it re-fretted so many times I've lost count."

"How did you come by it?"

"It cost me every penny I had at the time. A hundred bills to an old folkie who needed something softer. 'Cutz raaaight thru de bullsheeet!' as the folkie said. He was right. And it still never fails to inspire me. " He patted it lovingly before holding it at arms length.

I couldn't believe it when he handed the sacred instrument to me. "The action's like velvet," he said, with a smile, as if talking about the touch of cat's fur - or a woman's thigh. I carefully took it and gingerly touched the strings along the neck. Could this have been the guitar, I wondered, that produced the magical fade-out for the first time? Not the kind where a technician pulls down on the master switch and the music gradually fades away. Or, nowadays, where they simply press a button and the fade-out can be timed to the nearest thousandth of a second. No. This man's fade-out is famous because he can perform it live, time after time, unerringly, on stage in front of thousands of people. It's not synthesized. It's real. It's electrifying. It holds the audience mesmerized until it fades into nothingness. A vacuum in which a hundred thousand breaths are held, in anticipation, before going berserk. Applause erupting, screams and whistles exploding like waves of thunder, ripping around the stadium.

Sensing my awe his grin widened. "D'you play? Go ahead... it almost plays itself. It even fits right, like it's part of you."

Even though I'm no great guitarist I fumbled a straight-fingered bar chord to impress him. It was effortless.

"See? I didn't write the stuff at all," he chuckled. “It did. That old bastard wrote the music itself. I just wrote the lyrics and played along. Best hundred bills I ever spent. I'd sell this mansion if I ever had to. But not that. He stood and stretched. “Wanna drink, man?"

"Just a beer... thanks. " I was saved. As he left the room with that familiar strut I laid the Gibson back carefully against the wall. He returned in minutes with a six-pack and an opener.

We sipped from the long necks as we talked about his impending world tour, the *Farewell Tour*, said with a wink to the tomcat, to begin in a couple of weeks. And how this was also to be one of his very last intimate interviews. The list of questions in my notebook remained ignored but one niggled me. The Big Question. Perhaps this was the time to ask.

"The Fade-Out. What about it? Where did it come from?"

"Ah, yes" he began slowly. "I wondered when you'd get around to that again.” He laughed, bemused. “It's funny... nobody's ever asked me that before. Okay man, I've avoided discussing it all this time but maybe that would be the right way to go out. But I'll tell you on one condition. D'you agree?"

I nodded. "Yes." I had no choice.

"You'll get your scoop providing you promise not to write it until at least a year after the tour ends. About three years from now when I finally hang up the old Gibson here and retire." His large elegant hands spread in supplication before me. "God knows, I need to let it be known."

"But I must have this interview into the paper by tomorrow morning or I'll get fired."

"You have enough stuff to put the interview together for that, don't you?" I nodded again. "Now I'm asking you to do another story for me, after the tour, with this other information. If you agree you'll have a friend for life - and a story that every magazine in the world will want to publish. Can I trust you?"

"Okay. Sure you can. I give you my word. " This was too good to be true - only it was true ! The *Man* was asking *me* for a favour? He's offering *me* another story - and a scoop at that? Of course I'd go along with what he wanted. Apart from anything else he's offering me the biggest golden nest egg I'd ever have been afraid to imagine.

When we shook hands on it he took a faded black and white framed photograph from the wall. "That's Jimmy," he said. I looked into the smiling face of a clean-cut young man in, maybe, his late teens. His clothes suggested late 'fifties or early 'sixties. Who was Jimmy, I wondered? His name was vaguely familiar but I couldn't, for the life of me, think of where I'd seen or heard it. before. Just 'Jimmy' - nothing more.

"Jimmy started it all," he began gently. "He was The Man, not me. It was Jimmy who hit the first chord ... and he who invented the Fade-Out. " Pausing to open another bottle of beer he gave me time to study again the photograph in my hand. I was totally unprepared for this confession.

In thirty years of fame it was incredible that some more experienced journalist had not prized this secret from him. Then I began to wonder if it were true. If, in fact, the man's mind had begun to play tricks on him.

"So," I asked, "Who is this guy Jimmy ... and where is he now? I've never heard of him in the music industry."

He stared at me fixedly, anticipating my next question. "And you won't. He's been dead long since - even before the first single hit the charts. Jimmy and me, what a team we were ..." He broke off in mid-sentence, jumped to his feet, raising his hands to the ceiling "What a fucking band we would've been, man," he shouted, before letting his arms drop slowly to his sides. His voice became gruff. It cracked. I said nothing.

"Yeah, man. Jimmy didn't even make it to the first recording. And did anyone give a damn? No, only me. Poor sweet Jesus Jimmy. "

"What happened?"

"Leukemia. That's what happened." His voice became angrier as he expanded. "Fucking leukemia at seventeen. Not drugs or anything like that. The only *LSD* we knew about in those days were pounds, shillings and pence. And we didn't know too damn much about them either. We could hardly afford a packet of Woodbine."

He leaned forward and tapped me on the knee. No megastar now, just a man with a weighty story.

"Let me tell you something," he began, "Jimmy and me, we wrote the first album together. Yeah, man, we had it on tape before I even formed the band. Jimmy was long gone by the time we got into a studio.

"After he died, and 'Rock Steady' became a hit, I locked away all the material Jimmy and I had recorded together on the old Revox. He's always right there beside me in spirit. In every song, every chord. Every time I step out in front of the fans, Jimmy's there. Every time I set foot in the studio, he's there too. That's why you'll always read 'Special thanks to Jimmy' on the credits of all my recordings."

What a story! Of course I'd seen the name but never gave it a second thought. It could have been a technician or some other backroom hero. A quick glance at my recorder showed it was still going strong but the tape would soon need replacing. "Can you hold on a sec while I do this?" I asked. There was a panicky edge to my voice as I fidgeted with the new cassette. He threw his head back and laughed loudly.

"No hassle, man. I've waited thirty years so what's another few minutes ? Here, I'll get us more beer." The tape was running, the beer flowed, and the atmosphere was taut as an overstretched string. He continued to relinquish his secret, eyes blazing with excitement now.

"When I retire I'm gonna release it, d'you see ! There's plenty enough for a whole album ... and then I'm gonna step back and watch their goddamn faces. Yeah man, that'll be something else! The original famous first chord ... and the Fade -Out. Straight off the old Revox the way Jimmy invented it. That's how I'm gonna go out, me and Jimmy, stepping back from the mic ... F-A-D-E-O-U-T. Gone!"

A conspiratorial grin passed between us. I handed Jimmy's photograph back to him and he promised to lend it to me for the story. Watching him, momentarily lost in thought, I decided I liked the *Man* as much as I respected him and his music. In the space of a few hours he had become so much more than the Megastar I'd arrogantly come to interview. I switched off the tape, slipped it into my pocket and stood to go.

"Thanks so much for that," I said gratefully, holding out my hand to shake his. 'Your secret's safe but I must go now and write the piece for tomorrow."

He gripped my hand and held it. "Wait a minute, man. I've one last thing to show you." And with that he grabbed the *Gibson* and stuck that first chord. I watched in awe as he began to play the original version - especially for me. A privileged private audience. Only then did I suddenly realize what he was really showing me. Here, in close up, I saw the original has been a mistake! Nothing that would ever be found in any guitar lesson book. And that was the secret of it. A unique mistake.

I understood then how Jimmy, messing around for the first time, had struck what he thought was a regular chord but his fingers had misshaped it. Quickly fiddling with the notes to get it right. Jamming the two chords together, causing a fuzzy buzzing sound when electrified through an amplifier seemed to grip you by the back of the neck...

As the *Man* continued to play I could visualize them both in the early days. Two skinny teenagers, heads together, in that dingy old flat, messing. *"Hey! Wow! Howja do that? Gimme a go. Freakin' great. DRAAANNNNG!!!*

He sang the whole song, right through, to the end. And then slowly, with the *DRAAANNNG* of the final chord, began to edge his way out of the room, backing off without a creak or rustle, leaving only the sound of that magical chord hanging in the air like electrons of static reverberations.

I sat, spellbound, holding my breath.

THE TRIP

Robert was dozing in front of the fire when, with a little laugh, he suddenly sat upright in the chair. Maureen, sitting opposite, stopped knitting and turned her good ear towards her husband, waiting for him to speak. He chuckled again and settled back in his chair before noticing her looking across at him over the top of her glasses.

He waited while a vicious winter hailstorm, clattering against the windows, threatened to prevent him from being heard.

"I just remembered something," he said smiling, mildly embarrassed at being caught laughing at his own thoughts and apologetic for not explaining himself.

She knew his little ways - a laugh or cough to get her attention before launching himself into some anecdote. It could be anything from what one of the children did long ago on holiday to something as recent as paying the telephone bill. He told her about that yesterday. How he kept a long queue waiting while he searched through his pockets for the statement - only to be told kindly by the clerk that he had already paid it last week. This was happening to him more often.

But now, as Maureen waited, he simply closed his eyes and dozed off again without saying anything more.

He's getting old, she thought, and he's beginning to dote. It's such a pity. He was such a great one for telling stories but now all he seems to want to do is doze in front of the fire or mope around the garden shed. Well, let him sleep - at seventy-two he's earned the right.

Robert's sleeping form was hunched in the chair, arms tightly folded across his chest, thin nostrils quivering with each breath. She knew he would eventually tell her whatever it was he'd been thinking about. As she clicked her knitting needles into action again Maureen mused on how much Robert reminded her of their son, Michael, when he was a baby. The same shaped eyelids shut tight and fine wisps of hair sticking up on the top of his head. The thought brought a faint smile to her lips.

Robert and Maureen would be celebrating fifty years of happy marriage this coming spring. Michael, Jennifer and 'little' Robert were living in various parts of the country with families of their own and, any day now, there would be a phone call to announce the arrival of the first great-grandchild. They were as excited as if expecting their own firstborn.

Maureen felt the urge to talk but Robert was now snoring loudly. She missed their lively conversations which were becoming less frequent each day.

"The *divil* sweep him," she muttered aloud. "He's gone into his night's sleep and now he'll be awake half the night when we get to bed." She prodded him gently with her knitting needle. Robert woke with a snort.

"You were saying ... " she prompted. "Something you remembered?"

"Oh, was I?"

"You're getting worse," she scolded.

Robert rubbed the back of his hands over his eyes. "Aye, I suppose I am." He pointed at her knitting. "You're going great guns with that thing."

A web of intricate white cotton knitting spilled from the silver needles across her knees and into the bag at her feet. "Nearly finished and not a day too soon," Maureen replied. "I'm slowing down,"

"*Divil* a bit," Robert said as his eyes wandered from the christening shawl to the telephone behind her that might ring out the news any minute. "Any day now," he said, slapping his knees. "I can't wait." Robert loved children. The tiny puckered baby faces. The plump spongy little muscles. He indicated the shawl again. "How many's that now?" he wondered aloud. "Our three, Michael's three, Jenny's two, Robert's three ... and this one."

"Twelve" said Maureen who had no need to count. She had knitted all the family christening shawls since Michael made them parents for the first time in 1945 and now it had become a tradition for Granny Mo to make The Shawl.

Robert laughed and slapped his knees again. "D'you remember when you had to knit two of them at the same time? Michael's John and Jenny's Mary coming neck and neck."

Maureen gave a whoop of laughter, "Oho, that was a close one, right enough! I never thought I'd make it in time."

"But you did," Robert reminded her proudly. "You went at it like the blazes. I used to come home from the shop and cook our dinners so you could keep at it. You hadn't a minute to spare ... and I didn't do badly at all with the cooking."

"Well," said Maureen, cocking an eye at him, "You didn't poison anyone, anyway."

They laughed heartily as Robert threw a turf briquette on the fire causing sparks to rise and dance for a few seconds. He spread his hands to the heat.

"D'you know, if this weather doesn't let up soon ... I don't know what. Whoever is controlling it had better pull His socks up. God help the poor little nipper being born into this lot." Maureen shook her head, saying, "I've never witnessed worse." Then she glared at Robert who was settling back again in his chair. "You're not going back to sleep on me, are you?"

"No, just having a wee snooze, " he replied, closing his eyes. "A great-grandfather," he muttered aloud. "Who'd ever have thought it."

"We must have done something right," said Maureen gently.

Jeepers, thought Robert, I nearly let the cat out of the bag that time. I'd better watch myself in future. She'd have a fit if I was to tell her my surprise now on top of everything else that's happening. The baby, our golden wedding anniversary, the knitting. Knowing about the special holiday I'm planning for the pair of us, a second honeymoon - fifty years on - might be just too much for her. Mo's too old for all that excitement at once.

He stretched his legs and remembered their early days together. Even the war, shortages, rationing and almost no money wasn't enough to dampen our happiness. We still managed a small wedding and a week's holiday in Cork. Then the shop kept us going, just about ... until a few years ago.

Robert remembered his retirement party and the good advice he got from Sean Bartley, his life-long friend. Advice on investing the lump sum he got from the sale of the small shop. Now it had paid off, just as Sean said it would, and Robert had drawn it all out last week and spent the lot on his surprise for Maureen.

He had booked them in to spend twelve glorious days cruising the Mediterranean on the Penmouth Princess. He could hardly wait to show her the brochures. In the spring they'd visit several of Europe's most romantic cities - Barcelona, Marseilles, Cannes, Rome, Sorrento, Venice - all the places they'd talked about wanting to see. In the past something had always happened to upset their plans. This time, Robert promised silently, nothing would get in the way of their dreams.

He drifted into sleep thinking of the look on Maureen's face when he told her later. He saw her, in his mind's eye, knitting away with her skilled fingers on automatic pilot, checking him over the rims of her glasses. He felt the years dropping away as his imagination wallowed in the delights to come.

In his dream he was already slipping into warm soothing waters, far from this harsh Irish winter. He floated effortlessly through gentle blue ripples, turning on his back, feeling the sun's warm rays on his face and chest. Above him the sky was a transparent haze of sapphire.

A wonderful sensation of lightness carried him upwards and he began to expand with the vastness of it all. He became a great winged albatross, weightlessly floating through the blue crystal heavens while, down below, Maureen's needles clicked tirelessly. But what was he doing here alone? The holiday was for both of them. Maureen must share this experience too. Panic checked his flight.

"Mo!" he called, "Maureen?" But the knitting needles continued to glide through the white yarn. "Maureen!, Maureen!" he called again. Now he became frantic. I can't take this journey alone, he thought. We've been together too long. We've done everything together.

But Maureen was far below, unaware of her husband soaring high above her. Robert stretched out his arms to her. She was out of reach ... out of hearing ... and fading. He gave one last painful scream, "MAUREEN ... !"

She dropped her knitting and fell to her knees by his side.

"Robbie?" she called softly. "What is it, dear ... What ... ?" When he didn't answer she shook him wildly, digging her fingers into his shoulder. Robert's head fell forward limply. Maureen held it between her hands and looked, panic-stricken, at her husband's slumped frame. Her voice seems to come from far off as she screamed. "Oh, God!" she cried. "Oh God, no, Robbie, my poor Robbie!"

And somewhere, as if from the end of a long dark tunnel, a telephone rang.

Maureen shook her husband vigorously and shouted in a final cry of desperation, "Robbie, oh Robbie. The telephone …"

She stumbled across the room and grabbed the receiver. "Hold on. Please. It's Robbie. He's ..." She stopped, unable to go on, the struggle between life and death overwhelming her. She sat, hunched on the floor, looking back at her husband, and hearing Jenny's excited voice coming from the earpiece. *Oh dear God*, she prayed inwardly, *help us in our hour of need.*

"Robbie," she called softly, her voice breaking as starting to rise, imagining she saw a flicker of his eyelids, at the same time breathing into the telephone. "Hold on ... please," and, dropping it, crawled to her husband's side. "Robbie darling, it's the phone", she sobbed. Mary's had a little boy. Oh Robbie ..." Her voice broke. "Our great grand child. Oh, Robbie..."

Her husband's lips moved almost inperceptively. She leaned her ear to his mouth, straining to hear with all her being. "What is it, love?" she asked tenderly, cradling his head in her hands.

Robert's breath was a mere feather against her ear. "Thank God," he breathed, "I lived to see it."

"Yes," Maureen sobbed. "Yes, you did, love."

His head fell forward with a final sigh of breath and Maureen knew he could not hear her any more.

MAY'S SOLDIERS

She lined up her little soldiers. Blue. Pink. Spotty white. White with the red stripe. Blue for night time to help her sleep. Pink for the morning to help with her digestion. And the pretty spotty one in case that dreadful headache should come back. May had not needed to take this one for a while. She was glad. When the awful pain crept, like a hot niggling poker squirming across the top of her head, and crash landed between her eyes ... Ach ...!

She poked the last one with a fingernail. The capsule with the red stripe. Most important one of all. Her little striped soldier. Guardian of her wickedness. This was the chap who kept her calm. A General, standing proudly at the head of his troops. She placed him carefully in a pill box, hoping he wouldn't need to do his duty today, and slipped it into her handbag.

May had forgotten to take him on occasions. Sometimes after a particularly bad night's sleep, when she had ruined breakfast, couldn't find matching shoes and scattered clothes around the bedsit. When she slopped tea, marmalade, and bits of burnt toast over the Formica table top and had gone to work feeling rotten. She grimaced at the memory.

"Don't forget to take your little red soldier with you when you go to work," Nurse Cannon warned, her voice echoing in May's head.

Nurse Cannon. What a funny name. May remembered the picture of a cannon gun she had seen in a magazine. Nurse *Cannongun,* she called her after that. Hey! Hey! But not to her face. No! Oh no! Secretly to herself. Nurse *Cannongun!* Nurse-Cannon-with-her-guns had the authority of life and death. Nurse-Cannon-with-her-guns could give or take it all away. May sniggered as she placed two slices of bread under the grill and set the timer. The timer was clever. If she forgot it she burnt the toast.

One morning she burnt the whole sliced pan. She had slept badly that time, tossing all night, with mixed up scattered dreams that left her exhausted and frightened like a little child, unable to sleep again no matter how she lay.

In the morning, all doddering and fumbling, unable to think straight, wearing the wrong clothes and having ruined breakfast, she arrived an hour late for work. Before lunchtime all hell broke out in her and she ended up back in hospital.

May hated the hospital. The hard mattress, manhandling nurses, the straps, needles. Her mother hovering at the bedside, wringing hands, whining over and over, pinched little mouth squirmy like a creepy crawly. “What are we going to do with you, May. What are we going to do with you, at all, at all?”

And that look in her watery eyes saying you’re not like Tom and Maria or Deirdre and Paddy, with their nice jobs, nice baby, nice cars, nice tellys, nice gardens, nice dog, nice clothes and nice friends. Oh dear. *Ohdearohdearohdear*, May!

She didn’t get on with her brother or sister. On the odd occasions when she was invited to their homes, with all those nice things, she felt uncomfortable. They had made her feel unwanted, suffering her company for half a day, or an evening. Only Maria, Tom’s wife, accepted her. Her brother's obvious embarrassment annoyed May. But then, even as children, she was always in a row with him over something. Maria treated her like a normal human being.

Tom would not allow her to hold their baby. How she would have loved to cuddle it to her breast. But no. He said the baby was too delicate at the moment. Something or other about it’s lungs. Well, there was damn all wrong with its lungs when it was screaming for food. Maria pleaded with Tom but to no avail. Why shouldn't Auntie May hold the child? It was the first time May heard herself referred to in this way. She glowed in the new status as Maria thoughtfully bestowed the title on her. Auntie May!

But Tom shook his head even more vehemently just as she remembered him doing when they were children. No, to his cars, airplanes, and books. "No! May can not have them!" Her mother's mouth curdled. She shook her head in tandem with her son. "No! You can't have Tom’s new toy. You'll break it, you clumsy...!"

Now, here he was again, denying her pleasure from his newest toy. As she watched the tiny fingers clutching the air May felt excluded and crushed. Excusing herself, she rushed to the bathroom to hide her humiliation and swallow one of her soldiers. The spotted one who warded off tension when it gathered at the base of her neck like a timebomb.

When Tom drove her home it was always with the stereo blaring to avoid conversation. Only when she stepped from the car would he speak, in that patronizing voice, to ask the same boring question. "Will you be all right?" Would I be all right? Of course I bloody would. What does he think I am anyway? An invalid? It's not my fault if I get upset, and ill, now and again! Haven't I got arms and legs and other bits and pieces, all in good working order, just like him.

Then there was Deirdre and Paddy with their semi-detached snobby modern furniture. Her sister's husband took refuge behind a bottle of whiskey when she visited. With his mouth stuck to the glass he avoided meeting her eye and absolved himself from making even rudimentary conversation. Deirdre's conversation flounced between high falutin' fashion and hare-brained color schemes for the house. May didn't know what to say to her any more. She didn't want to visit them if she could help it but Mother dragged her along anyway.

If ever her red striped General needed to work overtime, it was after a visit to Deirdre and Paddy

May spread the beans across the toast with a fork and looked around her own little bedsit. Small as it was, she kept it spick and span.

Tom had never visited her here. Deirdre had never called. Mother had been three or four times, always complaining about the stairs, constantly out of breath when she climbed them. Then, stumbling for the old armchair in May's room, she would sink into its softness, wheezing and grasping. "Them stairs!" she invariably whined, "Oh dear, *ohdearohdear*! And nothing but this awful old chair to sit on."

The recollection made May wince. *Go away Mother, or I'll stick this fork in you!*

It was May's favorite chair. When she snuggled into it at night, her legs tucked up under her, to watch TV, the chair wrapped itself around her holding her warm and safe. A cocoon to sink into. Who needed more?

May rammed a forkful of beans and toast into her mouth and took a gulp of tea. She was in no hurry. There was plenty of time to get to the shop.

She enjoyed working in the bright shoe shop. And they called her Miss Murphy there. Miss Murphy. It was almost as good as 'Auntie May'. That was nice. It made her feel important. Part of her job was to keep all the shoes neat and tidy and free from dust which she did diligently. When Mister Curley said she was not to deal with the customers May was relieved. Strangers made her feel uncomfortable.

May liked neatness. Except when feeling unwell and then she did not care. That was rare now, ever since she had been discharged from the Home, and *Cannongun* had found her a flat and the job in the shoe shop. May had come to realize how good Nurse Cannon had been to her and, indeed, for her. The nurse was hateful only when she forgot to take the protection of the little red striped General. When things got out of hand. Then she was a terror! It was a busy shop, especially at weekends. The Manager, Mister Curley, was nice too. He treated her like everyone else. Always pleasant. A real gentleman even when there were no customers around. His kindly eyes spoke with understanding without the necessity of words.

Mr Curley reminded May of her father, or rather, of how he used to be. Before he stopped looking at her. When she was small he had played with her, as any father would, until she started school and they discovered she was a slower learner than the other children.

She might be a slow starter, the teacher reassured her parents, but she wasn't the only one. May understood none of this. She was only aware of the difficulty in keeping her attention on what she was supposed to learn. She could not sleep and cried all night, not knowing why or for what, and the pain in her head would not go away.

The slow-learners class was followed by a special school. By then she had lost interest in everything except numbers. She had liked the brightly colored figures, especially the big yellow eight.

Her duties at the shop included sorting out the sizes, ordinary and Continental, of all the lovely shoes. She understood the need to have them in their correct places and never made a mistake. Nobody knew the stock or the store-room like she did. That was her domain.

May worked with Martina, who was in charge of the Women's department, and the assistant manager, Mr. O'Connor, who was in charge of the Men's. She liked Martina but thought Mr. O'Connor was a *rat*. He was nice to them only when Mister Curley was around. May often thought of how she would love to give him a good thump on his wavy head and slice the smirk off his face. But the red striped General steadied her. And kept him safe.

Last time she forgot to take her General with her she found herself back in the clutches of *Cannongun*. It was a busy morning and Martina had asked May to get a particular style of shoe from the store-room for the woman she was serving. On her return May and the customer recognized each other as fellow patients from the hospital. As they began to chat May became aware that Mr. O'Connor was glaring across at her. Nervously, she began to shred the tissue paper from the shoes, unaware she was still holding it. Tiny white flakes fell around her feet as she continued to talk.

If Martina didn't mind her having a chat why should he? It wasn't as if she was interfering with anyone. This was someone she knew from before she ever worked in this shop.

In the end her friend decided not to take the shoes and left. Martina went to assist a prospective customer as May began to tidy up. Mister O'Connor appeared at her side in a fuming temper. "Look at the mess you've made!" he hissed. "And you lost that sale! Don't you know you're not supposed to interfere when Miss Higgins is serving a customer? If I was Manager it would come out of your wages ... "

"Well, you're not the Manager!" said Martina, coming quickly to May's rescue.

"If Mister Curley was to know ... ," fumed Mr. O'Connor.

“And who’s to tell? She was a friend of May's," Martina retorted.

“No," he insisted, "in my shop a customer is a *CUSTOMER*, not a friend!”

May stood motionless as anger flashed between them. Terror and confusion raged within her until they merged into a spuming outburst. Suddenly the whole shop seemed to tumble down around them. Shoes flew off the racks. Shelves emptied their contents onto the floor, scattering shoes in every direction. How long this avalanche lasted she did not know.

The next thing she knew was arms encircling her, holding her, forcing her down. Screams and shouts echoed through her and then *Cannongun* and the others were there, bundling and coaxing, surrounding her, speeding along to the hospital and the needles and straps all over again.

When she recovered Mister Curley was forgiving and took her back. “Just lucky nobody was hurt," he said gently. May sensed the underlying kindness masked behind her boss's stern set of eyebrows. A real gentleman.

She knew that Martina was glad to have her back again by the way she laughed and pretended to be upset. “There was me, having to run back and forth to the store for my own orders, and knowing where nothing is. We couldn’t manage without you, could we?”

But Mister Dermot *rat* O’Connor had not welcomed her back. Instead he ignored her, pointedly avoiding her, for the first few days. But then he found it impossible to keep running to the store every few minutes and still retain his notions.

Some day, some sweet day, May had often thought, the same man would trip over his highfalutin' notions and break his scrawny neck.

Gradually he had begun to ask for her assistance again. But now, months later, something had happened which disturbed and frightened May beyond her comprehension.

Last Saturday had been a particularly busy day in the shop. A week-end sale. May ran frantically to and from the store to fetch, "a pair of size nine brown brogues, or black court shoes with a little bow, or can you find a half size smaller, or bigger, Miss Murphy, No! ... ankle boots or knee boots ..." and on and on while everyone was kept busy with the constant stream of customers.

When she was having difficulty finding the right color on the Men’s shelving Mister O’Connor came into the stockroom behind her. Hurrying her up, confusing her, putting undue pressure on her, as if she was not already stretched to the threshold of her limit. He pushed roughly past her, rummaging among the boxes, scattering shoes and swearing under his breath. Blaming her for the mess he had created. “Why can’t you keep this place in some sort of order ... Huh?” The offensive breath, hot on May's face, disgusted her. She wanted to hit him but held herself in check. Her heart thumped in her chest as tears welled behind her eyelids.

“Well...? Huh...?” he demanded, hissing through his little pointed teeth.

As May's tears overflowed she remembered the General tucked away in her handbag which hung under her coat on the back of the store-room door. Only the General could help her now!

"The General!" she cried, attempting to push Mister O'Connor away. "I must get the ... "

He shoved her roughly back against the shelves. "You'll get nobody, damn you! What are you trying to do ... get me into trouble?"

Suddenly his hateful hand was rubbing her face, smearing the tears into her skin. And then, with one hand on her neck, he began to paw the front of her dress.

Struggling to escape his molesting fingers she fell over the mess he had created. He turned and raced out, laughing, leaving her sprawled among the debris; her skirt rucked up shamefully, arms crossed defensively over her breasts. May sat there, in confusion, trying to rub out the feel of his filthy grasping hands, until she remembered where she was.

She scrambled to her feet in panic. Hurriedly she began to put shoes back in boxes, not caring where, any box, any shoe.

Must tidy up, she thought desperately, sponging her wet face with the back of her hand. Must put everything back. What if Mister Curley saw? I'll be thrown out. Back in the hospital under *Cannongun's* clutches. It's not fair that O'Connor can get away with it, just because he's in charge of the Men's. May reached for her handbag and raced to the toilet.

Rarely had the little General to work so hard. Never had the soothing presence in her veins been so welcome. Had she struck back at the assistant manager instead of recoiling she would surely have been out on her ear this time. Mister Curley could not have been expected to be so kind a second time. And she wouldn't blame him.

Over Sunday May tried to put the incident out of her mind. She tidied the bedsit, mended some clothes, watched television, took her pills and slept well.

But now it was Monday and she would be at work within the hour. Mister Curley was at a Trade Fair until Wednesday and Dermot *'rat'* O'Connor was in charge. She would have to spend most of the day in the store room, rearranging the mess of Saturday, and he knew that. He would be there to supervise it.

What if he gets at me again to-day? What if he begins to sneer at me? What if he grabs me with his slimy hands? The horrible little *rat-face* of his.

She finished her tea and took the cup, saucer, and plate to the sink. The General stood alone on the Formica table top. May took the dish cloth and ran it under the hot water.

I'll just have to be on my guard today. But if he touches me ... if he touches me there ... ! Already she could feel the slimy hands... Ach! She shook her head violently to rid it of the horrible image.

She wiped the crumbs off the table taking care not to disturb the General. She paused, cocking her head to one side, smiling at him tenderly. What, she wondered, would happen, if she didn't take him to work to-day? Supposing she went without his protection?

Picking up the little tablet between her fingers May gazed thoughtfully at it for a few moments. Then, with a roguish grin, she returned it to the centre of the table. A wicked thought presented itself to her mind. Yes, she decided, she would face the coming day alone, without the protection of her little 'General'.

Wrapping her coat and scarf around her, she headed for the door, pausing only for one last look at the 'General', who stood to attention, all alone, on his kitchen table parade ground. Closing the door softly behind her she bounded down the stairs. Today she would deal with that *rat* O'Connor in her own simple way... And God help anyone who tried to stop her.

GRACE

The news that Grace was pregnant ricocheted around the store like a marked bullet. Grace Minnelli, of all people!

It lopped from counter to counter, floor to floor, missing nobody. Butchers grinned. Bakers nodded and giggled. Checkout girls raised eyebrows and threw knowledgeable glances to each other up and down the line. By the time the first tea-break filled the canteen it was common knowledge from the Manager to the Yard man.

Poor Grace! Stupid Grace! Silly Bitch!

Beautiful Grace. Grace Minnelli, only child of an Irish mother and Italian father, had inherited the beauty of both races. An invigorating beauty that took the attention of every male who set eyes on her and was the envy of every female.

The men in the store were no exception even though they came in contact with her every working day. Visiting sales representatives and merchandisers did their utmost to meet her by arranging to work nearby, wherever she was situated that day, paying scant attention to their own company products. The other girls were jealous of all the attention she was attracting.

And now Grace, whom they regarded as a goddess among mortals, was rumoured to be pregnant. Everyone pondered and speculated and wondered and pondered and speculated all over again.

A gaggle of ears surrounded Jenny Fogerty who had spread the news until the supervisor, Miss Hall, barking like a terrier among pecking crows, scattered them back to their own departments.

Normally Jenny was one of the last out of the changing room. This morning it was curiosity, rather than a reluctance to work, that held her back.

Distressed sounds from a locked cubicle suggested there might be a juicy story to liven up her day. Just as she decided she could not wait any longer the loo door opened. Out came Grace tentatively, her face drained of all colour, looking frightened and fragile.

“You're not sick, are you, Grace?” Jenny asked with feigned friendliness begging for gossip.

Grace stalled in shock, not expecting to be confronted by anyone, particularly Jenny. Of all the people to see her! Flustered, she wiped her mouth and chin with a tissue, buying time.

“God, you look awful,” sniggered Jenny. Grace shook her head in silence, flashing a look of hostility at Jenny, as she lurched to the wash-basin for a splash of cold water to try and bring some colour and normality back to her face. But in that look Jenny saw her dilemma and covered her glee with a look of mock horror.

“Jesus! Grace! You're not, are you...? Jenny clapped a hand over her gaping mouth and bounded from the room.

Grace felt she could have strangled her work mate. And cut her own tongue out for not thinking fast enough to tell the nosy biddy to mind her own business. In her present state of mind and body she was no match for that vixen. Now her distress was revealed to the busiest bush telegraph on the West side.

If only it was Fran who had been waiting outside the cubicle instead of Jenny. At least she would have been sympathetic and discreet. But Fran had been ticked off a number of times lately for dallying and was trying to get back in the Supervisor’s good books by being prompt in her time-keeping.

Then again, maybe this abomination had not been visited upon her. Grace found herself pondering on her possible predicament in Biblical terms. Was she with child.? Had she begotten? Had the seed been sown in her.?

Dammit! What if she really was pregnant - going to have a baby. A bastard! So, what the hell was she going to do about it? At eighteen, in her first job, she had no plans to get married, or to be a single parent, or to have anything whatsoever to do with babies or children for a long time to come. There were too many things she wanted to do first, too many pleasures to be enjoyed, a vast ocean of life yet to be explored.

If this was so, what about the disgrace to her family? A vision of her mother's face, disappointed and pained, passed through her mind until it was shattered by a sudden image of her father's anger. His Italian blood and defiled honour would surely react with violence. He could kill her and the guy who did it to her.

Maybe it wasn't true. Perhaps these symptoms were due to something else. Like the stress of being stuck in a job she hated.

Early on she realized the futility of constant shelf stocking and managerial preaching. Assistant managers aping their bosses annoyed her. It was as if selling peas and packet soup has become a new religion. This was not what she had in mind for the remainder of her life. She wanted something more. What exactly 'something more' was she hadn't yet discovered, but she knew it wasn't this.

One sunny afternoon, as Grace placed what seemed like the millionth can of beans on a shelf, a group of exuberant students jostled past her. Their carefree attitude made her wonder what life would be like had she gone to university. If only she had never made that silly promise to Fran. Maybe the Prince her father had always said was waiting to marry her, would be the next man to wander along the aisle, she thought with irony.

And now, if this thing was inside her, it could ruin whatever chances she had. Nausea continued to erode her denial. If only something or someone could solve this problem or make it go away.

Why had she not confided in someone before, Grace wondered. Why had she not told Fran? Goodness only knows. They hadn't been together as much as usual lately. But that wasn't the real reason. She was terrified of saying it out loud - of even admitting it to herself - in case this made it real. It could not happen to her - the honey-pot around which the bees buzzed. Surely her carefree days were not so easily numbered.? She couldn't have been that stupid.

Grace's decision to skip college and go to work in the local shopping centre had, at first, made her father slap his forehead and spit, "*Basta, que causa!*" to the ceiling, his dark eyes wild. He argued passionately that this was no job for his *Princessa* until gently reminded by her mother that he had also gone against his family's wishes. Besides, she soothed, Grace would soon see the folly of her decision, and what difference would a year make.

What her parents did not know was that the basis of Grace's decision lay in a secret promise to Fran, her best friend, and she was determined to keep her word. While still at school Fran had pleaded with her not to allow them to be separated, they were such great friends, they would do everything together. Get jobs. Get husbands. Children... Grace, in her innocence, readily agreed to this flattering plea. Both girls began work together at the supermarket on the same day.

But now she could be pregnant and Fran wasn't and the man responsible was certainly no prince.

It had all started as bravado on her part during a party at a friend's house. The usual kind of teenage rave-up. Parents away for the week-end. It was exactly like the last hundred parties she had been to. The music was fine, the beer was okay, the dope she didn't use, but the guys were the same lot that seemed to turn up everywhere swarming around her like mosquitoes. As Grace tolerated their attentions she realized how bored she had become with them all. Then she saw him.

Leaning against the wall, drinking a can of beer, paying no attention to her, was a guy she did not know. He was tall thin and dressed in black. Although he was not the best-looking man in the room he had an interesting face. As she studied him, Grace decided it was his expression that intrigued her. A look of brooding arrogance set him apart. His long elegant fingers held a beer can as if it were a goblet.

Grace watched him curiously, because, even though he was much like all the rest of them, in age and experience, he had an aura of self-assured solitude. She decided, in an instant, to do something she had never done before. Can in hand she approached him confidently.

Thinking back on it now made her want to jump off a bridge. She must have been drunker than she imagined, because she allowed one thing lead to the next. He had simply acknowledged her sudden appearance with a nod of his head. While continuing to follow the conversation around him he drew her closer to him. Yes, he was different and mysterious. She felt part of it all but as if she were on the outside looking in with him. He seemed older and more mature than the others and a lot more self-assured.

After a while he asked her if she smoked. She said no but would not object if he did. Which, looking back now, sounded silly.

He grinned and whispered that he was going out the back to roll a number. Did she want to come? Grace shrugged and followed him out.

At the back of the house he smoothly rolled a joint. Grace had never seen anyone do this so well before. The ceremonious way in which he put it together, the deftness of his long elegant fingers, and the measured way he ran his tongue over the papers, fascinated her. It was as if he were presiding over some mystical mediaeval ritual.

Then he lit it with reverence and took a long drag, holding his breath, before allowing a stream of pale smoke to filter from his nostrils. He took a second pull before handing it to Grace. She looked at the strange cigarette, wondering what to do, never having smoked before. Sensing her indecision he raised her hand to his own mouth and took another long toke. Then, lowering his face to hers, he kissed her deeply until she could taste the sweet pungency of the drug on the back of her throat. He smiled and drew more smoke before kissing her again, this time letting his tongue play around the inside of her lips. Her head began to swim as the taste of tobacco and hash mingled with the kiss. Grace began to feel as if she were floating, light and feathery....

Suddenly he was above her somehow and she wondered at the smell of oil and earth, while he unzipped her jeans. She became aware of his fingers caressing her hot moistness. Her head and body ebbed and flowed in slow timeless rhythmic pleasure until a sharp pain invaded her reverie. Rapture melted into confusion as this inflicted hurt registered, stealthily and deliberately, on Grace's muddled thoughts. The cry forming in her mind bubbled towards her throat as his salty palm covered her lips. A deep growl in his chest stifled her protest as she felt his pleasure vibrate through her.

Somehow she got home and to the safety of her bed without encountering her parents. How, was still a blank in her memory.

It was Fran who later warned her about the dark stranger. He was definitely to be avoided if she wanted to stay out of trouble with the Gardaí. Grace admitted only to a bit of a grope and a wee smoke.

Since the party the friends had seen little of each other after work because Fran was spending more time with her new boyfriend.

The door of the rest room opened.

"Are you all right?" asked Miss Hall, her voice firm but concerned. Grace dabbed her face with the tissue. The supervisor stepped inside, closed the door and leant against it. "Are you all right, Miss Minelli?" she asked again.

Grace nodded, unable to speak. At first she cowed, mistrusting, expecting a reprimand, but soon realized Miss Hall's concern for her was genuine. Up to now their only conversation had been to do with shop matters, but as Grace felt strength and kindness emanating from Miss Hall she was momentarily tempted to appeal to her compassion and confide the whole story to her. But fear choked her.

"Are you feeling sick? Do you want to go home?"

Grace was grateful for the calm voice which was not trying to hound her back to work. She turned to face her superior.

"You don't look well at all." Miss Hall gestured to a chair, "Here, sit down." The order was spoken without reprimand. "Can I get you something?"

Grace sat. It was a relief. "I'll be all right in a minute," she mumbled, her stomach beginning to heave again. She could feel the blood draining from her head. Grace put her head between her knees hoping that it would help. A light touch rested on her shoulder.

"Would you like me to call a doctor?"

God, no! thought Grace, straightening slowly, willing the nausea to go away. "No. Thanks. I'll be all right."

"I think the best thing would be to get a taxi and take you home."

Grace nodded silently, her face ashen. Miss Hall continued, “It’ll pass - the sickness, I mean - but have you told anyone about it?"

"About what?"

"Have you told your mother?”

"My mother? Grace shook her head in terror.

Miss Hall bent to comfort her. "I think when you've talked to your mother about it, it won't seem so bad. You're not the first and you'll not be the last. You have to face it. And once you've discussed it fairly and openly with your parents you'll be in a better position to decide what to do”.

Grace was dumbstruck. She couldn't believe what she was hearing. The reality of what Miss Hall had said burst, like a bomb, in her brain. Any hope she had that this problem was imaginary suddenly collapsed within her.

It was as if she had stepped outside herself and seen not Grace the *Princessa*, but Grace the *Poverina* - the slut! Hatred for this newly decrepit self burned inside her. A bundle of crumpled features, cheap overalls, disheveled hair, slumped shoulders. And now, with this thing growing inside her...

The sight of this neat self-assured woman who blocked the door filled her with resentment. Realizing that Miss Hall knew the sinister truth she herself had refused to acknowledge sent Grace into a stifling panic. The urge to flee and find a hiding place almost suffocated her. Nobody could help her now. She was lost. Her mind raced down a long dark alley, pursued by horror of her mother's anguish, her father's anger, and her own disgrace.

She felt a hand tighten on her shoulder and, looking up, saw Miss Hall reach out as if to embrace her. Frightened, trapped like a hurt animal, she pushed the arms away in anger.

"You don't understand," Grace screamed in her supervisor's face. Then, roughly shoving the woman to one side, hurled herself at the door.

"You don't understand at all," she screamed again in despair, stumbling from the locker room, down the stairs, and out of the building, head down, avoiding the penetrating looks of the others as she burst out into the sharp light of day.

The world was different now from how she had always imagined and, for her, it would never again be the same.

PARTYING

"I want to go out Gerry, I want to party." Kathy pummeled the air with her hands in despair. "I'm fed up sitting doing nothing. I need some excitement."

Gerry watched her coldly through a haze of smoke.

"This... shaggin' sitting around is killing me. For *Chrissake*, Gerry, it's the longest night of the year. Everyone is out having a good time. And what are we doing? Sitting on our arses, talking rubbish."

Gerry continued to stare. His tight lips worked slowly from side to side. He chain-lit another cigarette. "You're the only one saying anything," he snorted.

"Exactly," Kathy exploded. "That's just what I mean. And it's damn boring."

Gerry blew a cloud of smoke over her head. A shred of tobacco stuck to his lip. He pushed it off with the tip of his tongue and spat it away. "You can go out if you want to ..."

"There's nobody stopping me, huh? Is that what you mean?" Kathy finished the sentence for him. Instantly she knew it was a mistake. But it was too late. Like a shot he leapt to his feet and, grabbing her by the shoulder, yanked her off the sofa and pushed her into the street.

"Look! Up there," he hissed. "See that. Big orange moon, right?" He twisted her head upwards. "Two more nights and it'll be full. Midwinter, my arse. You haven't a clue what it's all about. You don't appreciate these things." He jerked her head. "And see that big purple cloud. Beautiful. Huh?"

"It's grey, Gerry. It's grey." Tears of frustration welled up in her. He continued to speak as she twisted out of his grasp, "That's the problem with you Kathy. You see everything as grey."

The cigarette dangled from his bottom lip with puffs of smoke accentuating each word. "But it's not. There's colour everywhere. All you have to do is open your eyes. I've tried to - educate you. Make you see what's around you ..."

As he rambled on, her frustration blocked him out. It was as if Gerry had melted before her eyes and was replaced by a smarmy preacher with a demonic glare in his eyes.

What is happening to him? Kathy wondered in anguish. This latest trip of his has me shattered. He sits there, ruminating, day after day, claiming to see colour everywhere. Sitting on his arse smoking his way through his Dole every week! He'd be better off back on the booze. But even that is a big issue with him since he was barred from every pub in town for head-butting anyone who dared to disagree with his crazy theories. And he won't drink at home. More craziness. Is he too proud to go to the off-license? Or too stupid, maybe? He refuses to discuss it and he won't let me go either. He's a demon when he's drinking but a fool when he isn't. Now he's just plain crazy.

The drone of his voice pervaded her thoughts.

"...grey clouds. Grey sky. Grey friends. Politically grey. Spiritually grey. I've tried to show you Kath, but it's your brain. Your brain is grey. Can you not see that?"

She attempted to push past him but Gerry dug his hands into her shoulders and planted her in front of him. "Listen, Kathy ..."

She squirmed.

"You're hurting me."

He relaxed his grip and she spun away from him. "If it's grey it's grey!" She spat the words at him. "I don't care. You're stone mad Gerry FitzGerald. I don't have to see everything the way you bloody-well see it. I just want to go to the pub and have a bit of fun. Meet a few people. Have a few drinks. What's the harm in that?" She waved her arm at the sky. "It's not up there for me. Bloody great balls of fluff." She pointed down the moonlit street towards the bright lights of town. "That's where it's at for me." Then the tears came. “What the hell am I doing with you, anyway?” she sobbed, “what the hell am I doing ...”

“You know right well what you’re doing with me,” Gerry replied scathingly.

Kathy shook her head. “I don’t know. I don’t know anything any more. I just want to meet a few friends. Have the *craic*. A few drinks.”

“Alcohol’s a bad vibe.”

“Oh, not that again, Gerry.”

He shook his head slowly. “You’ll never learn will you. You want to kill your brain cells, huh? You want to rot your gut with that ... swill? Fill yourself up with chemicals? You want to act the eejit. Talk all that rubbish with your bullshitty so-called friends. Not while you’re living in this house, you won’t.”

“Well then maybe ...”

“Well then maybe ... what?”

“Well then maybe I’ll just go anyway.”

“You’re a big girl now. You can go where you like. But we’ve talked about this and you know what I think."

“I know what you think Gerry. But what about me and what I think?”

He shooed her with a wave of his hand. “Okay, okay. Go. Go ahead. But you know the consequences.”

“Damn you, Gerry.”

As she stepped away he caught her by the arm. “Kathy, look, you know what I think, right? I’ve just tried to show you. When did I ever try to stand in your way?" He smiled crookedly. "When did I ever stop you from doing anything, huh?”

Kathy’s fists flailed the air. She wished she had the courage to actually hit him. “No, Gerry, you’ve never stopped me from doing anything. But then I’ve never actually done anything. A bit of encouragement wouldn't have gone astray. Did that ever occur to you?

As her voice rose to a scream curtains jerked open across the street. Silhouettes appeared briefly in windows to confirm it was only the FitzGeralds at it again.

Gerry pulled her towards the house. “C'mon, we’ll talk about this inside.”

“No!” Kathy shrugged her arm from his grip. “You don’t make sense any more. We’re just going 'round in circles.” She pointed at the jerking curtains. “And I don’t give a damn about them either. We’ll shaggin' well stand out here under your bloody purple cloud and talk about it. And whoever likes can open their moldy curtains and watch.” She turned, screaming at the houses opposite, “and it's probably more bloody interesting than what's on telly ... but then I wouldn't know, would I? That's another thing I'm not allowed to bloody-well have."

Gerry lunged at her but this time she evaded him, prancing out into the middle of the road, where she began a manic dance of rage.

Leaning back against the doorway, he watched her through slit eyes, lighting another cigarette. He flicked the match away and moved quickly towards her, attempting to hold her. But it was like trying to embrace a pneumatic drill.

“Stop, Kathy,” he said softly, "C'mon now. Cool it. OK."

The unfamiliar tenderness in his voice stopped her in mid-dance. She glared at him distrustfully.

“Come on, Kathy. Let’s go back in the house." He reached out again to hold her. She backed away.

“No, Gerry. Leave me alone.”

“Kath, Kath, please.”

“Go away, Gerry.”

Without a word he took a step back, swung his boot, and kicked the legs from under her.

With a smack her face hit the concrete and blood spurted from her nose. A silent agonized scream tore through her stunned brain. Blood dripped onto the road as she heaved herself on to her knees. Her shoulder ached and her left hip felt as if the skin had been torn off. Behind her the door slammed shut. Then she was on her feet, rushing away, cursing the pain. Damn him!

A woman's voice called softly from a darkened doorway. "Are you all right, Miss?"

Kathy ignored it. Of course I'm all right. Just a broken nose, ha, bloody ha. Thanks for your concern. Damned if I'll give the nosy old bag the satisfaction ...

She strode on regardless of the stream of blood soaking the front of her blouse.

Suddenly Gerry appeared at her side. "Come on, Kathy. Home."

She strode on, his footsteps marching in time with hers. "Kath. Home."

"No."

"Kath."

"No!."

Gerry gripped her arm to slow her down.

"Okay," he said, "we'll go to the pub if that's what you want."

More blood splattered as Kathy shook her head in disbelief. Stopping abruptly she turned to face him. "Don't be ridiculous Gerry." Flecks of blood showered the front of his shirt through the spluttered words. He peered down at them in disgust, thumbing his nose, in a steamy silence. She froze, waiting for the blow, but it did not come. Instead his hand dropped and swung loosely at his side.

"Look at the state of you! I thought you wanted to go to the pub?"

Kathy sniffed a few times in an effort to clear her nose. "I still do," she replied angrily. "Only you can't."

"Who says so, huh?" He took out a handkerchief and reached to wipe her face. She stepped away, angrily, thinking. So I'm losing a bit of blood. Well, no big deal. I'm a woman amn't I! She made no attempt to wipe it away herself.

"First you want to go to the pub and then you don't. As usual you're not making any sense, Kathy."

She attempted to laugh in his face but it came out as a snort. More blood splattered his shirt. He ignored it.

"You're playing games again, Kath. Here, clean your face."

She brushed aside the proffered handkerchief as if its very whiteness was a reminder of what he withheld from her. "Go away," she said, "I don't care. Just - go - away."

Gerry cocked his head to one side, as if looking at a bird with a broken wing, wondering whether to take it home to nurse, or stamp on its head to end its misery. He rubbed his nose between thumb and forefinger again, shrugged and, turning abruptly, strode away.

Disgust welled up in her as she watched his belligerent retreat. Lousy swaggering bastard, that's him all over.

Gerry turned, and seeing her still standing in the same spot, waved her on. "Get moving then," he called, his voice echoing down the street. "Go to your pub. See your friends. Fine. But when you come back ..." He thumbed his nose at her, sneering.

Kathy strode up the street, malice boiling through her veins. Gerry's words pursued her. "And when you come home guess who'll be waiting, huh? No, not your yappy friends. Who'll be waiting to wipe up your vomit? Not your yappy friends, huh?"

Kathy carried on. But where was there to go? She could never go back. This was the last time. She'd had enough. Enough of his crazy raving. The stupid endless arguments. His fists. His tormenting. In some ways it was worse before his enforced fanatical anti-booze trip, anti social trip, anti *everything* trip. But now he was just plain off-the-wall - Mad.

But where was she to go? She had no friends anymore. He'd seen to that. Her family didn't want to know her. Gerry had fixed that too.

And now she was in no state to go to the pub either. She didn't know what to do. She decided to keep walking. To the ends of the earth if necessary. Her stubborn pride taking her through the longest night of the year. Another dismal night in her life.

But she knew she would go back. How many times in the past had his blows sent her scurrying to some bleak refuge? How many hours until her weary legs retraced her tracks to his craziness? Some dark corner of her being needed that mad sick bastard. They needed each other.

But what she could not fathom in her present befuddled state - was why?

THE NEUTERING

Nicholas woke with a start. Had he dreamed the splintering sound or was it real? Lying still, holding his breath, he strained to listen in the darkness. All was silent. He fumbled sleepily for his glasses on the bedside table and peered at the illuminated dial of the clock. Four-thirty A.M. He lay down again, pulling the bedclothes tight around his neck, but another crashing sound brought him bolt upright. This time there was no mistaking it for imagination or dream and it came from the far side of the house where Nicholas's studio was situated. The completed paintings for his forth coming exhibition stood there ready for collection in the morning.

"Damn that cat," he hissed, leaping out of bed. "I'll kill him." Nicholas snapped on the bedroom light and hurried through the old darkened house switching on all the lights as he passed through the rooms.

How did that infernal animal get in again, he wondered. I must have left the window open. But I'm sure I didn't. Jock, was a large tomcat and never allowed in the studio, since he had taken to knocking over pots of paint, for sheer devilment, his owner imagined, and when reprimanded, began to spray the place with his overpowering stink. That was when Nicholas decided to have him neutered. Now, it seemed, the old tom was having his revenge.

"Jock, you're a dead duck," he roared, swinging open the heavy studio door and reaching for the light switch. But a sudden movement from the far corner of the room stopped him and, in the same instant, he heard a click and a white beam from a powerful torch swung across the room, catching him in its arc, momentarily blinding him. He froze in terror.

Nicholas felt the blood drain from his head and, feeling as if about to fall to the floor, reached out to steady himself against the doorjamb. Oh Christ, he thought in agony, my greatest nightmare realized before my eyes. Someone has broken in and is wrecking my paintings. Is this real or is it just my greatest fear manifesting in a dream..? But it was no dream.

Then he felt his courage return as the initial shock turned to rage and he took a step towards the flashlight. A low mocking laugh stopped him in his tracks. Terror filled him once more. The laughing continued and suddenly the reason for it dawned on him. He stood motionless in the beam of light as he visualized himself dressed only in his pink striped underpants; his old narrow chest and spindly arms and legs exposed.

"What do you want?" he shrieked in a cracking voice. He could just make out the large menacing shape dimly illuminated by the moonlight from the windows and realized he would be no match for the intruder if attacked. At the same time he spotted a pair of cat's eyes glinting at him motionlessly from a corner under the shelving.

"Jock, you useless cat," he wailed. "Why aren't you a dog!"

"Shut up," the intruder barked, taking a step towards him, raising the heavy torchlight threateningly, its beam flashing across the ceiling before coming to rest on his face again. In the instant the light was out of his eyes, Nicholas recognized something familiar in the interloper's shape, the small rounded head on broad shoulders. And the voice, young, with a broad city accent.

My god, he began to recollect, its a boy from one of the inner city projects I ran last year. But which one, I was involved in so many? And which boy? If I could only remember his name it might save me. I could talk to him. It might calm him down when he remembered me.

But then all hope abandoned him as he remembered who this youth was. He had been the most troublesome of the lot. Awkward and leering, he had sneered at Nicholas and everything he tried to teach. The paint brushes were like useless twigs in this boy's thick hands. He knocked over easels and splattered paint on the other boys work laughing scornfully at their protests. Not one of them could handle him. He was an overgrown hulk of a child in schoolboy's clothing. An unmitigated bully that nobody could control until the unexpected happened and finally settled him down to work, revealing a budding talent. Even if it was only for depictions of outrageous characters in lurid colours.

The boys name rose to the tip of his tongue but stuck there like a glob of glue and would not ring out. It was connected to a famous painting, he knew it well, but his terror at the advancing hulk froze it in his memory. *Stars. That was it. Yes, lots of stars. Oh, damn, what was it?* And then it came to him in a bolt. The 'Starry Night', by ... he racked his brain but the name of the famous artist would not come to him. It was the painting that had changed his assailant and set him off, painting furiously, causing Nicholas to remark on his sudden and inspired talent. To encourage and show his approval, he had casually invited the young artist to visit his studio sometime, as he had with other talented students, to try and help them.

But, on the last morning of the project, the day of the exhibition, when within an hour patents and local dignitaries were expected to view the culmination of the project's work they arrived and discovered to their consternation, every piece of work daubed mercilessly with monstrous stars. Someone had broken in during the night and committed this savage attack. Weeks of painstaking work was ruined. The culprit was blatantly obvious and made no appearance. But there was no proof...

But now he had turned up again like a terrorist in the night and was caught in the act repeating his former crime.

And then, in a flash, the bully's name came back to Nicholas. The same as that crazed Dutch artist ...

"Vincent ... !" he croaked, his voice breaking. “Yes. It's Vincent! Isn't it?” But the boy made no reply and advanced menacingly.

Nicolas stretched out his hands beseechingly in defense. “Oh no! Oh God no...” he gasped, as his eyes, pinned to the circle of light on the tip of the heavy torch, watched incredulously, as it swept in an ark and came crashing towards his head.

Jimmy jumps out of bed on the first 'blip' of the alarm clock at eight A.M. He takes a cold shower, brushes his teeth and shaves carefully, trimming his thick, black mustache. A firm slap of aftershave gives the finishing touch. Then, dressing meticulously, he decides to bypass breakfast and his first cigarette of the day, wanting no unnecessary baggage of ingestion or inhalation to slow him down. A light stomach and a clear head, he tells himself, is what he needs most to face Josie.

By eight thirty he is out of the house, his steady stride marking his determination. For, this morning, Jimmy Henterson, height five foot five, is on his way, to steal his own child.

This time Josie will be caught well off her guard, he speculates boldly, when I knock on her door at eight forty five. She will imagine the postman with a parcel or telegram. She won't be thinking of Jimmy. Her sleepy eyed look of surprise will turn to shock as I march past her straight down the narrow hall into her pokey kitchen. Her protests will follow me, hoping to shoo me out as quickly as I came in. Let them. By then I'll have taken my stance with my back to the window, feet firmly planted, at the furthest point from the front door. From this vantage point, with the morning light at my back, I'll enjoy watching her tussle with the dregs of sleep.

Reveling in these heroic images of himself he strides purposefully onward to her door.

He knows Josie is never at her brightest in the morning. At this hour her well practiced sarcastic tongue will be caught napping. Her morning ritual of chain drinking mugs of murky black coffee will not yet have unlocked her caustic phrase book. Before the kettle has boiled for her first, Jimmy will have swooped, like a General in a dawn maneuver on his enemy, and vanished with his prize.

Josie, confused and startled, will explode in his face like an old blunderbuss, hissing and scratching like a wildcat protecting her brood. But she won't dare to touch him. This he is confident of. He will stand his ground, a slight bemused smile on his face, surveying her over the debris of her life. The clutter of yesterdays encrusted dishes. The overflowing ashtrays. The roaches from last nights joints. The grimy table-top. The sticky linoleum. Chairs askew. Baby clothes abandoned. Stale air.

Jimmy feels well fortified against all this with his bellyful of fresh morning air, flexed muscles, and oxygen pumping through his brain. Josie will be no match for him. The best she will come up with, from her acid arsenal, at this unearthly hour of the morning, he reckons, will be something like, 'So what rat hole did you manage to crawl out of this morning?' But even her sneer won't be up to measure. Jimmy will just shake his head pitifully at her. "You're the rat Josie baby. This is your hole. And you are caught."

"Fuck you. Jimmy."

"Oh. I'm sure you can do better than that," he sneers.

Josie lights a cigarette, inhaling deeply, preparing to hurl a new obscenity at his head. But he carries on.

"Before I do what I came to do I want to tell you a few truths. First, about your attempts to raise our child ..."

He doesn't get to finish. It's as if at that moment a tornado hits the kitchen. Knives flash by his head. Spoons bounce off his shirt front. Forks prick his jacket. Dirty plates smash on his raised protecting forearms. Every piece of cutlery and crockery that is on the table between them targets him. Josie showers him relentlessly. He ducks, bobs, sways, and jumps, in a wild protecting dance. Then, as suddenly as it began, it stops. Josie's hot stale breath is popping in his face. Her voice is a wild screeching.

'YOU POOFED UP BAG OF RAT SLIME. HOW DARE YOU. HOW DARE YOU COME INTO MY HOME AND ATTEMPT TO LECTURE ME ON HOW I REAR MY CHILD..."

Jimmy remains calm, having fortified himself against her outbursts, and reminds her quietly. "Our child."

"MY. CHILD. MY. CHILD." Josie screams, her body pulsating with the rhythm of the words.

"Our child Josie."

Jimmy's composure, despite the remnants of Josie's previous nights dinner clinging to his clothes, remains intact. He continues as calmly as before. "Josie. You're fooling yourself. You're my wife and little Jimmy is our child. It's as simple as that. You ran out on me Josie. You stole our child. You can't do that. You won't get away with it. I won't let you. We've got to rectify this ridiculous situation before it goes to far."

Then she begins to laugh. A wild raucous throaty sound which Jimmy hates. Once, he thought it sexy, a great turn-on. And it was, until Josie began to direct it at him. Now it is so full of venom he can feel it tearing at his skin like paint stripper.

"Josie." He raises his voice to get her attention, waving his hands at the devastation in the kitchen. "This is no way to rear our son. You're slovenly, lazy, and you've no discipline. Once you come to terms with your - inadequacies - your shortcomings - we'll be in a position to rectify it. Save our marriage and our son. Basically, Josie, you've the mentality of a tramp. But you're not a tramp. You're far too intelligent and too well educated to be a tramp."

He watches her vigilantly as she stockpiles his words, twisting them and maneuvering them into line, to hurl back in his face. Nevertheless he continues. "It's as if you've fallen down a hole and refuse to help yourself crawl out again."

Josie begins to mime his words, her hands slowly clawing the air, as if trying to drag herself up a muddy slope. Jimmy can see the malice underscoring the feigned grimace of effort on her face, but he blocks it and carries on.

"You're taking advice from the wrong people. You're ruining yourself with caffeine and dope and living in this pigsty. It's impossible to have a straight conversation with you. If you're prepared to admit - to yourself most of all ... "

Josie throws her head back and rolls her eyes to the ceiling until all he can see is the murky yellow of her eyeballs.

Jimmy hurries on, undaunted. "... that what I'm saying is true. Then we'll be able to, at least, begin to talk about it and salvage something of what we had. If not, then I have no alternative but ..."

Josie claps her hands together in a slow rhythm, cutting across his rant, one hand falling limply on the other. "Good for you *Sunny-Jim*," she smirks. "Who wrote this latest speech of yours? I'm impressed."

She rescues the kettle from the floor and, plugging it in, favours Jimmy with a leering smile. "Would you like some coffee? You must be thirsty after all that - bullshit," she says, slamming two cups with broken handles on the table, inviting him to sit. "So you want to play the Truth Game? Fair enough. Point for point. Tit for tat. My tit. Your tat." Her raucous laugh, flavoured with her stale breath, explodes once again in his face.

Jimmy sits, maintaining a poker face with effort, refusing her offer of coffee. He will not play the fish to her bait. He must keep his eye on his objective; his sleeping son upstairs.

"This is not a game, Josie."

"Oh, come now, Jimmy, we're not in the mood for games, huh? But then you never were the 'games type'. Never one of our 'sporting young men,' so to speak." She settles back in the chair, cocking an eyebrow, waiting for her latest volley to take effect.

But he remains silent, determined not to get drawn into a slagging match with her.

Josie recognizes this and changes tack. "Right. Okay. No games. Just facts. Do you really want me to spell out for you again why our, so called, marriage came to an untimely end? You say I'm lazy. Sloppy. And, all right, it's no secret, I smoke some dope and drink too much coffee and I'm a bit untidy. Big deal! But your downfall was the booze. And surely, Sunny-Jim ... Okay, no name calling. Sorry ... I forgot your type have sensitive natures ... Have you forgotten already what you did - or should I say - tried to do, to me? Is your memory that short? Come on now. You can't be that forgetful."

Jimmy knows what she is hinting at. “It’s not true,’ he says flatly.

“You mean I'm still imagining it. The way you were carrying on? The strange stink off you?”

“It’s not true.”

“You said you weren’t well. Remember. You came in from the pub. At five o’clock in the morning. You came to bed. There was a strange smell off you. You told me you had been sick. But it wasn’t that kind of smell. No. The smell I’m referring to comes from another place. Down under so to speak. Do you still want me to spell it out?”

Jimmy warns himself not to be taunted by her affront. He feels his bile rising but fights it down, because he knows if he doesn’t, he will feel like killing her.

“Josie. I am not ...” he begins forcefully. But he cannot continue. He cannot say the thing she is accusing him of - ‘queer.’ Josie keeps a straight face, watching his efforts to stay in control, but beneath it she can see the murderous hate in his eyes.

“Okay. Okay," she says hurriedly to sidestep him, her voice matter-of-fact, but tempered with irony. "Just a few minutes ago you asked me to admit some truths about myself. You said ‘admit to myself first’. Right. Now what about you? Are you prepared to admit ‘to yourself first', what you know to be true? What I know. What half the town knows? Come out of the closet, Jimmy, then we can all make a fresh start. Stop fooling yourself.”

“It’s not true,” he protests vehemently. Then, realizing that he is loosing his temper, continues in a mollified tone, conceding. “Yes. It's true. Some of my friends are gay. There’s no wrong in that. Is there? And, yes, I am very fond of Thomas. There’s nothing wrong with that either. And we did get drunk together. It was the only way he could pour his problems out to me - to anyone. And yes, we were up in his flat, until five o’clock in the morning. And what if somebody saw us with our arms around each other in the street. We were dead drunk. We’re the oldest of friends. Have been since infants class. And I was sick that night. Sick as a dog ...”

Josie swallows a mouthful of coffee and glares at him. She has heard it all before and is sick of it. "Jimmy-boy. Stop deluding yourself. The week after you and Thomas got dead drunk together he came out and admitted to the world that he was gay. He also admitted that he was in love with you."

"It's a lie. Thomas never said that."

"But I don't give a damn who's in love with who. All I care about is, that you did it with him and then you stumbled home and *drunk as a skunk* tried to do it with me. That, *Sunny-Jim*, is the crime accused. Your problem is not that you did or didn't do it. Your problem is that you were caught out. Your problem is that you were as guilty as hell but you wouldn't admit it."

Jimmy's head begins to shake from side to side, slowly, defensively. He doesn't remember much about that night except that he was very drunk and violently ill. Thomas couldn't remember much either about what took place after they left the pub nursing a bottle of whisky. He did remember there was a smell of sick in his bathroom the next morning. But he didn't know whether it was his or Jimmy's. He categorically denied that he ever said he was in love with Jimmy. He confided that he did love him, but certainly not in any sexual way. Jesus Christ, he protested, Jimmy was his best and oldest friend. He loved him like a brother.

If he did seduce him, and God forbid that he did, if there was any seduction, from either side, it absolutely wasn't intentional. That night is a great black blank. But, yes, he did come out shortly after and admit he was gay. He went to Josie and told her all this. But Josie didn't believe him. Or for reasons only known to herself *wouldn't* believe him. He was saddened and sickened by what had happened to their relationship, blaming himself. He was devastated by it.

At this point Jimmy and Josie realize they have come face to face against a blank wall. It is not the first time it has confronted them. One of them must break the stalemate. But who will make the first move?

For a few minutes they remain locked in their individual isolated speculations across the battlefield of the kitchen table.

Josie uses this reprieve to make more coffee, offering Jimmy a cup. A small gesture of truce? He refuses, not wanting to involve himself in her coffee drinking ritual, knowing it is a ploy to make him hyper and lose direction. And, also, he decides, to accept anything from her hand now, would be a show of weakness. There is only one thing he wants to take from her - his child. When he does - and he feels the moment approaching stealthily like a cat stalking a trapped mouse - that is what will break her. He awaits his moment of triumph, savoring it in silence. Josie, sensing this silent maneuvering, moves to block it, continuing to chip away at the armor of his respite.

“I heard Thomas is going to move in with you.”

Silence.

“Well.” She shrugs to show him that she is now only trying to engage in normal conversation. “It’s a big flat you have. And you told me you don’t like living alone.”

Silence.

“I can’t see what’s wrong with that. After all, he is your childhood buddy. You’d get on well together. The only problem is that he’s a liar and so are you. But then perhaps two lies will make a truth.”

As she banters on, she eyes Jimmy guardedly, watching for a danger signal, some shift in his fabricated composure. A tightened fist. A clamping of his jaw. But there is none. Just his conceited wall of silence.

With a sudden movement, Jimmy springs to his feet, taking her by surprise. Josie ducks instinctively, expecting a blow, but instead he swiftly skirts the table and races from the kitchen.

Josie, rallying speedily, thinking he is leaving, swings around in her chair, and aims a parting shot at his back. “Leaving so soon. Huh? Just when we were getting on so well - I don’t think! Call again soon. Don’t slam the door.”

But Jimmy runs up the stairs, taking them two at a time, expecting Josie to try and stop him. She remains seated with her hands warming around her coffee cup, a broad smirk on her face, listening to him clomping from room to room. What does he expect to find, she wonders. A slumbering lover? A stash of drugs?

Minutes later he has returned and stands menacingly in the doorway, fists clenched furiously, with a wild look in his eyes. Josie has never seen him so vicious before and covers her shock with a manic laugh. “Enjoy your tour of inspection? I hope the sight of my exotic underwear didn’t upset you too much?” she says, tearing her attention away from his glaring eyes to her coffee cup.

“Where’s the baby?”

“What baby?”

“Don’t get smart with me,” he hisses and takes a step towards her.

“Oh I never was smart. You were always the smart one Sunny-Jim.”

“Josie. I’ll ask one more time. Where is little Jimmy?”

“I sold him,” she says, shrugging nonchalantly, testing the waters of his rage, as she stands to top up her coffee, thinking, that if he threatens her further, he will get it full blast in the face. “Y’know what I’d love?” she continues, keeping the edge out of her voice, as if musing to herself. “A real percolator. God, I’d love some real coffee. This instant shit is killing me.”

Jimmy seethes, watching the ripples of suppressed laughter playing along the muscles of her shoulders. He can contain himself no longer. Throwing himself across the room, he grabs her by the shoulders, and shakes her like a rag doll.

Josie, taken completely be surprise by this newfound swiftness that she never witnessed before in him, drops the boiling cup, scalding her hand. She cries out in pain, berating herself for not being quick enough.

“Where - Is - The - Baby,” he roars, punctuating each word with a violent shake.

Josie, struggling to extricate herself from his grasp, musters her forces. “I hired him out," she yells, beginning to laugh at her own wisecrack. "There’s a great trade in hiring out babies at present. So many childless women. I have to make ends meet somehow, y'know. Because you are no damn help."

She struggles harder, trying to release herself from his agonizing grip, only wanting to get away, knowing that if she were to fight him physically, she would tear the eyes right out of his head. The joke is on Jimmy, she realizes, now that she knows his reason for coming this morning, and that is the only thing stopping her from returning his violence. Did he think for one minute he would get away with it. That she would fall for his crazy nonsense.

"WHERE IS HE?"

Jimmy's nails dig deeper into her shoulders, but instead of groans of agony, he is surprised to hear peals of laughter beginning to bubble up through her. Sensing the momentary relaxation of his clutching fingers, Josie finally wrenches herself away from him, and, spinning out of reach stands, laughing hysterically, at the mixture of frustration and rage on his face.

"Our little darling is gone off hiking with his palls," she squeals, enjoying her new invention, clapping her hands gaily. "Oh. You should have seen them. The little lambs. Their little nappies waggling behind them."

Jimmy takes a menacing step towards her. Josie sidesteps and retreats around the table. "No. I'm joking," she continues, fighting to control her hilarity. "No. I was jokin'. He's gone to visit my mother. Or was it your mother. Anyway, he's in his granny's. No. I tell a lie. He's in hospital. He fell down the stairs. In the middle of the night. He was looking for his daddy. Or was it his teddy? I don't remember. I was asleep. He climbed out of his cot all by himself. He's a clever little lad. But then how would you know..."

They circle each other around the table. Josie knows already that Jimmy is beaten. The crushed look in his eyes is a clear giveaway. Already he is winding down like a clockwork toy. His shoulders drop and he stops the chase, leaning on the table, deflated.

Josie stands in the centre of the kitchen, arms folded, studying Jimmy through weary eyes. Poor *Sunny-Jim*, she thinks. When will he ever cop-on that this has become a meaningless charade. If he could only see himself now, crumpled and old before his time, useless, and positively mad. Playing out this stupid game for the past umpteen years. Pretending we were ever married. Pretending there was ever hope for us.

What a pathetic creature he is. Three months living with him all those years ago was more that enough to realize what an insane, twisted, imagination he had. When will it finally break on his deranged brain that we have nothing for each other. His past delusions were childish and harmless, even fun at times, because I could always beat him at his own game. Why I ever indulged him I'll never know. I must be as mad as he is.

But this newfangled fantasy, this preposterous illusion, that we have a child, takes the whole box of biscuits. Sheer lunacy. And now, this sudden violence ... It's not a game any more. It's dangerous territory. But this is the end of it. Enough.

Tomorrow, she promises herself. Tomorrow, I will pack my bags, put a torch to this pig sty and vanish from him and this madness for the last time.

SOMETHING TO SAY

Frank slid into a quiet corner seat of his local pub and, glancing around to make sure he would not be disturbed, took some loose pages from his jacket pocket and smoothed them on the table. Ballpoint poised, thoughts concentrated, he began to write . . .

Ken, perched on a high stool at the counter, sniffed and without taking his eyes from the newspaper, rummaged in his pocket for a dry tissue. At the same time he hoped to encounter a stray five pound note. No luck with either. Sniffing again he decided he needed another pint.

He wiped the bar counter with his sleeve, making sure it was dry before putting down his newspaper and slid off his high stool to go to the gents for some tissue.

Margo, sitting on the stool beside him, caught his sleeve urgently. "Kenneth?" It was the first word she had uttered in the past half hour. He had forgotten she was there.

"Pardon?"

"Kenneth, are you leaving?"

"No." He sniffed again. "Just going to find something to blow my nose."

"Kenneth, wait," she rummaged in her shoulder bag and thrust a tissue at him, "I have something to say. To tell you, actually."

He took the tissue from her and blew noisily. "What d'you mean?"

"Kenneth, I don't quite know how to say this so I'll just say it straight out. I love you. I mean ... I'm in love with you." Her eyes, dark and intense, burned into his.

"You're what? I say! " He jolted back from her in amazement, "Margo! "

"I'm in love with you, Kenneth. I simply had to tell you. It's been . . . oh, I don't know. " Her eyes brimmed with tears.

"Oh, God! " Shocked, he looked around appealing for help, but there was nobody except the bar man at the far end of the counter engrossed in a magazine. It was a quiet Tuesday afternoon.

Ken snorted into Margo's tissue again, although there was no need, then stuffed it into his pocket. Picking up his newspaper, he turned it over to check for wet spots, suddenly needing to keep his hands busy.

"I'm sorry, Kenneth," Margo said in a small voice, "I've shocked you. I'm sorry." She stared at her feet, embarrassed.

He folded and unfolded the paper nervously, paused, then slapped it on the counter. "No need to be sorry, Margo. But, really, you can't be serious?"

She began to fiddle with the lapel of his blazer, turning it over, then patting it flat again. "I'm afraid I am," she replied, with a nervous laugh, giving the lapel a final pat. When she raised her eyes to his they glistened with longing. "Have been for the last six months," she continued. "As a matter of fact, ever since Easter."

"Easter?" Ken did not understand.

"My birthday. Remember? You gave me the biggest Easter egg ever. It was a foot high, tied with an enormous red bow ... the most gorgeous thing..." Her words trailed off.

"I had an income then," Ken said, trying to bring a tone of sanity back into the conversation. "I could afford it, dear girl."

Margo shook her head slowly. "No," she sobbed, "it was more than that."

"I had bags of money. An Easter egg is only . . ."

"No! " Margo cried, raising her voice to block out his

dismissive tone. "It 's not 'only' anything! It was special to me. Very special."

Ken balked at this new assertion and turned away in embarrassment hoping she had not been overheard. The bar man caught his sudden movement and looked up. "Would you care for another drink, sir?'

"Yes, please. Jolly good idea. Thank you, John," Ken replied, flinging his words across the room to shoot down Margo's last utterances that, to him, still buzzed in the air like bluebottles.

While having Jim's attention he quickly mimed a scribble in the air behind Margo's back. John sighed and frowned, the weight of a thousand unpaid-for drinks etched in the furrows of his brow.

"Certainly, sir," he said, placing a glass under the tap, and reaching for the 'slate' on the shelf behind him. He nodded towards Margo. "And for the lady?"

"I'm fine, thank you," Margo replied, quickly covering the dregs of her gin and tonic with her hand. I'd love another drink, she thought, but I'd better not at the way things are turning out. Another one would make me weepy.

But Ken, over-riding her thoughts, called another for her.

"No, no, really," she protested. But John was too fast and was already placing the drink . . . . . .

A huge dark frame suddenly loomed over Frank as a hairy square hand scooped the pages from under his pen leaving a jagged rip under the last line.

"What the ... hey, George! " he protested as the other man, pint in hand, plonked down in the seat beside him clutching the sheaf of paper .

"Let's have a squint at what yer scribblin', Frank, m'lad." George's voice boomed around the pub. "Now. What have we here, young Chekhov?" he grinned wickedly, settling his bulk and fending off Frank's attempts to retrieve his manuscript.

“Hey, George, gimmie them back. It's nothin' to do with you.”

“Hold yer horses a minute. What's the big secret anyway?”

George pushed him back into his seat and began to read. “Relax, will ya,” he growled, as Frank gave one last grasp before sinking back in frustration.

Angrily he watched George’s black eyebrows working up and down as he scanned the first page, gathering momentum as he read through the second, until finally they were flapping like a nervous blackbird in flight.

“*Holy Mother O’ God*!” George exclaimed as he finished reading. “Ya can’t write that! It makes no sense at all.” He waggled the pages in Frank’s face, glaring at him, eyebrows closing down on the bridge of his bulbous nose like two thorn bushes in a gap.

Frank lunged, grasping for the manuscript, “C’mon, George, gimmie them back. You've no right ...”

But George, fencing him off with a huge arm, slipped the pages onto the soft seat beneath him, scrunching them under his weight. He took a long swallow from his pint and slammed the glass on the table. “Wooa there, Frankie-boy.”

“Look, it’s none of your business.”

“Well now, ” George declared, folding his arms and settling back, smiling widely, revealing the gaps in his disintegrating teeth. “And, if it’s no concern of mine, whose concern is it?”

“That's not the point.”

“Aren’t you a good friend of mine and amn’t I concerned about ya?" George asked benevolently, head to one side, eyebrows knitting and purling. He indicated to the captive manuscript, “And this poor girl ... whatshername?”

“Margo.”

“Margo . . . that I’m sittin' on. What about her?" He grinned wickedly then became serious again. “Sure no self-respectin'' woman would ever do what you’ve just had her doin'.”

“George. It’s only a story. I’m making it up.” Frank explained slowly, in a voice he reserved for idiots.

“I see,” George nodded his scraggy head. “Making it up, is it? But aren’t we all aware that nothin' can come out of the imagination unless it was put in there in the first place?” He glared fixedly at Frank waiting for confirmation.

Frank glared back in silence. George continued.

“Now, tell me. About this poor unfortunate woman. From whence came the information yer relatin'? In other words, on what corner-stone of personal experience are ya basin' yer epistle?”

“George, I told you, it’s pure fiction. There was no woman. And, anyway, I can write what I damn well like.”

“Granted,” George conceded. “But ... ” he held up an oratorical finger, “who will read it?" He paused dramatically, thrusting himself at Frank. “And furthermore, who will want to read it? And, more importantly, who will believe it?” His eyes swept around the bar seeking an extended audience but only finding the bar man.

“That’s not the point,” Frank began, but George held up a hand to stop him.

“That's exactly my point, young man.”

At this George jumped to his feet, snatching up the pages and, in two long strides, was leaning on the counter calling the bar man. “Donnie, come here a minute, will ya.”

He slapped the manuscript down on the counter. Frank leaped after him, grasping for it, but George’s huge bulk warded him off. As he handed the pages to Donnie, George said, “Have a squint at that and give me your unbiased opinion.”

“No! Please . . .!" pleaded the mortified writer.

George picked Frank up like a rag doll and planted him on a bar stool. “Give the man a chance, will ya,” he said with a demonic smile. “Sure aren’t we all friends here. Aren’t we only trying to lend assistance to a budding genius.”

They waited while Donnie slowly mouthed the words silently as he read. George stood, arms folded like Sitting Bull, an expectant grin on his face, as Frank smoldered on his stool.

At last Donnie came to the end.

“Well?” George demanded.

Donnie shrugged, “It’s all right, I suppose,” he said slowly. “But what happened next?”

“All right, is it!" George exploded in fury and pounded the counter with his fist. “Next, is it! Sure, what could happen 'next' but yer man would run outa the bar as fast as his legs could carry him.”

“Well . . . ” Donnie frowned then glanced at the pages again. He drew himself up like a barrister in a courtroom about to make a moot point. “There’s this bit here . . .” He flicked the pages in his hand. “No bar man could serve a gin and tonic that fast.”

“I - I can fix that,” Frank said quickly. “It’s only a first draft.”

George snorted and shook his head like a rampant stallion.

“Y’see,” Donnie continued, “he’d have to wait for the optic.”

“That’s rubbish!” George bawled, leaning over the counter, his face inches from Donnie’s. “Tell us about the woman!” he hissed. “In all your experience did any woman of any race, creed, persuasion or denomination ever do the likes of what young Frank here has made this one do?" George sucked in a lungful of air and continued. "To profess her love so unreservedly in open daylight, to a sniffling buffoon, who obviously hasn’t shown the least bit of interest in the poor creature, except to present her with the extravagance of ten Euros worth of chocolate egg?”

Donnie was not perturbed by George's bombastic outcry. He shrugged and pursed his thin lips. “Oh I don’t know,” he began thoughtfully, surveying the length of the bar, reviewing in his mind the endless parade of characters who embroidered his premises, “You get all sorts in here, y’know.”

Frank bristled with the excitement of a puppy presented with a biscuit but George patted him down. “All types, yes,” he hissed, snatching the pages from Donnie. “But, as for this nonsense, sure no woman in her right mind would . . .”

Donnie's upraised hand abruptly silenced him. The others waited impatiently as the bar man gathered his thoughts. “Yes,” Donnie said finally, “you see, maybe she wasn’t in her right mind.”

George turned on him contentiously. “In that case," he roared, "all eccentric, erratic, and screwball expurgations of a writer’s characters could be simply explained away by declaring them, insane. No.” His arm slashed through the air cutting Donnie's argument to shreds. “Unacceptable. Unjustifiable. Crap.”

“So, what do you suggest?” Frank asked innocently.

“I’m not suggestin' anything," George snorted. "You’re the writer. It’s up to you to solve the problem. Not me.”

“But even as an experiment . . .”

“Experiment is it? If it’s experiments you’re looking for then look at Barthelme. Even our own Joyce. Or Abramowitz. But if you want the pure story check out Maughan.”

“He’s right,” Donnie said, scratching his head sagely.

Frank and George both looked at him incredulously. They had never known the bar man to read anything except the headlines in the daily newspaper. Perhaps they had misjudged him after all. Could he be a closet literary intellectual? Frank wondered.

“Aye. I have to agree with George,” Donnie continued as they waited, open mouthed, for his opinion. “She’d be mad to give herself away like that. Women are cleverer, you know. They’re more subtle, like.”

“Baldertripe! ” George scoffed.

“There was yer one used to come in here," Donnie continued, ignoring George's outburst, "she sat beside this fellow who used to read books, on that very stool you’re sitting on." He indicated Frank’s bar stool. “They never spoke a word to each other, that I ever heard, anyway. He had his nose stuck in the book ignoring her. She just sat. For months they came in here. Then one day I heard they were married. Just like that."

"So?"

"What . . . ?"

"Oh, I don't know how she done it. Too subtle for me." Donnie shrugged his narrow shoulders and scurried off to serve a customer who had just come in.

"Well that was no help. No help whatsoever," said George, sucking air through his teeth and glaring at Donnie's retreating back. "All the same I suppose it gives you something to think about." He turned abruptly, picked up his pint and strode off to the other end of the bar, leaving Frank to pick up his crumpled manuscript.

"Well thanks a lot," he muttered to Georges retreating bulk, ironing the creases out of the pages with the flat of his hand, folding them carefully into his inside pocket. Picking up a discarded newspaper he fished in his jeans for money. He needed a drink. There was only loose change but not enough of it. He gestured to Donnie for a pint and mimed the slate.

"It's on the house," Donnie grinned, nodding knowingly, when he finally placed the drink before him. "You need it after that fellow," he continued, inclining his head towards George who was now engrossed in conversation in the farthest corner of the bar.

Frank supped his pint and surrounded himself with the newspaper, pretending to read. He was fuming. That is the last time I'll ever write anything in a public place, he promised. No matter how brilliant or how urgent it is. Even if it's tearing my guts out to be written. Little wonder writers hide themselves away in pokey rooms. *Never again!* He vowed and buried himself further behind the newspaper lost in thought.

Almost immediately a scratching sound on the other side of the paper disturbed him. Frank gave the pages a sharp shake as a warning, thinking it was George returning to torment him. The disturbance continued. This time he ignored it. The scratching became tapping; then rustling. Infuriated, Frank dropped the paper ready to pounce, but it wasn't George. Instead, Adele, his former girlfriend stood there with a huge smile on her scarlet lips.

“Frank," she began sweetly. "*Darlin'*. . . ”

“What d'you want? I'm broke.”

“I don't want anything," she replied with mock indignation, pursing her moist lips as if to kiss him; the sweet aroma of her lipstick filling his nostrils. "You look awfully cross. Don’t be cross Frank.”

“I’m not angry,” Frank replied testily.

“Fraaank," Adele purred. “I don't know how to say this, Frankie. It's something . . . something I’ve wanted to say for a long time.”

She stroked the lapel of his jacket lovingly with long slender fingers; her doe-like eyes caressing his face.

He brushed her hand away. “What are you up to?”

Then it dawned on him.

He recoiled from the intensity of her mocking gaze and toppled off his stool in his haste to get away.

“No,” he shrieked, "Oh no." And racing in panic from the bar, remembered that other Easter, the real Easter and a real Easter Egg. The one he had bought for Adele. Had she spilled the beans..? *The scheming bitch! How could she have done this to me.* He cringed with embarrassment, dodging the mocking eyes of George and Donnie as he bolted for the door and out into the street, their raucous laughter snapping at his heels like a pack of wild dogs.

CRASH

Susan dragged her knapsack from the boot of the car that had taken her on the last leg of her journey and dumped it on the pavement with relief. Digging a crumpled pack of cigarettes from the depths of her old leather jacket she gave the driver a paltry wave as he maneuvered back into the onslaught of traffic. For the past two hours she had sat glaring at the *No Smoking* sign on the dashboard and parrying his chat-up banter.

The stiffness of the past two days traveling by bus, ferry and car, still gripped at her bones. She lit the cigarette and inhaled hungrily, surveying the outskirts of her home town, remembering that when she had left two years ago it was reported as being the fastest growing city in the west of Ireland. But to her eyes now, it resembled a cartoon painted village, basking in the mild spring sunshine, after the grey immensity of London.

The fresh tang of the sea, drifting in on the light breeze, surprised and exhilarated her, filling her with memories. Throwing the cigarette away she stretched and, hoisting the rucksack onto her back, decided to walk to her brother's flat. The two mile walk across town would give her time to prepare. He did not know she was coming. Neither had she told her parents. She was not ready to face them yet.

Jimmy's flat was as she remembered - cold and dull. His welcome was similar.

"What do you want?" he snarled when he opened the door. His sour face, head and shoulders above his sister, glared down on her.

To hell with you, Susan thought, swallowing hard to force back the anger forming on her tongue, I might as well be some ragged beggerwoman. Her first reaction was to turn and march away, maintaining her dignity, but she forced her feet to stay put. Mustering as much courage as she could she grinned up at him.

"Hello little brother. Long time no-see."

Jimmy's arrogant expression did not budge. Susan thought for a moment he was about to slam the door shut in her face.

"I suppose you'd better come in," he said stiffly and stepped back.

Susan brushed quickly past him before he changed his mind. "If I'm not putting you to too much trouble," she muttered, sliding the knapsack off her shoulders and dropping it in the hallway.

Jimmy led the way into the living room and settled himself at the table which was piled with books. He did not ask Susan to sit so she slid onto the chair opposite him. He eyed her warily over the stacked texts.

"So," she ventured. "Still studying?"

Jimmy made no reply. He picked up his pen and fiddled with it nervously for a few moments before throwing it down again distractedly.

"D'you want a cup of tea?" he asked, his belligerent tone suggesting she should say no and leave.

"Yes please," Susan replied, wondering how long she could maintain her forced cheerfulness, but she couldn't help adding, "Good old Irish hospitality. Huh?"

Jimmy ignored her sarcasm and went to the kitchen to fill the kettle. He came back with cups and cleared a space for them, carefully rearranging the books.

"So what brings you back," he asked.

"You're not delighted to see me ... no?" A look of mock innocence lit up her face.

Jimmy stared at her for a minute, his head cocked to one side, his mouth a tight thin line. He shrugged noncommittally.

"It's all the one to me," he said, and went to the kitchen to make the tea, calling back over his shoulder. "You can come or go as you please. But I hope you don't expect me to put you up." When he came back with the teapot and milk he said in a tone of finality. "You can't stay here. I'm cramming for my finals. I don't need any interruptions."

Same long string of misery, Susan thought. She was his elder by a year. A fact that had always galled her brother.

"I'll be as quiet as a mouse," she said, smiling sweetly, attempting to humour him. But she knew it was a waste of energy

"There's lots of hostels," he replied flatly.

Susan lit a cigarette and blew the smoke into the air above his head. "I've no money."

Jimmy shrugged, "That's your problem." He fanned the smoke out of his face. "And stop blowing smoke over the food."

Susan was about to protest that a lukewarm cup of tea was hardly a meal but she remained calm. No point in getting up his nose, she warned herself, I need a place to stay.

Eventually she talked him into letting her stay the night. She was anxious to cross the first hurdle - Jimmy - before broaching the tougher course - her parents. And, she needed to find out how things stood now, two years after she had been thrown out of their home. But Jimmy was reluctant to talk about them, brushing aside her probing with shrugged monosyllables.

When Susan pressed him harder Jimmy stormed at her, "Leave it Susan. You've done enough damage. Two years you've been gone. Do you honestly expect to solve or change anything by reappearing now?"

Susan balked at his persistent hostility but clamped down on her own anger. It had nothing to do with him, she fumed silently. She was the one forced to flee when her father, professor of philosophy at the university, continually angered by her reluctance to attend lectures, and the rock band crowd she hung around with, had finally lost control and attacked her like a demon, raining blows on her. In her fury she had picked up a bread knife from the draining board to defend herself, warding him off. But it was her mother's actions Susan had never been able to fathom. Her own mother, wrenching her away and flinging her screaming out the door. It was true her mother had been drinking heavily at the time but that didn't explain why she had turned recklessly on her own daughter.

Susan had returned now, optimistic, that time and hundreds of miles separation would have eased aside the barriers. She was worn out, firstly from two days traveling in cramped busses and cars, and now, from Jimmy's reticence to offer her a civil word. Reluctantly she asked him for a key and left to look up some old friends. She had not kept in touch with any and was regretting it now.

On her way into town Susan made a snap decision to ring her father; it was still early enough to catch him at the University. She had no idea what she was going to say to him. That, she would have to play by ear when she heard his voice. Dialing his direct number she listened anxiously to the signal buzzing down the wires.

Suddenly her father was on the line, his voice snapping sharply in her ear. "Yes. Scannell here."

Susan faltered. "Hello dad. It's Susan."

"Who...?"

"Susan. It's me, dad."

"Oh...!"

She waited for him to continue. She could hear feint noises on the line as if her father was chewing unspoken words. Testing them. When he finally spoke again his voice was guarded. "Where are you ringing from?"

"Town. I'm in town."

"Town? Here?"

"I'm staying in Jimmy's. I just got in."

Again a pause.

Susan held her breath, listening to her father's breathing coming and going in her ear. It seemed to her as if he was shaking his head from side to side.

"With James?" he said after some time, "I see." She could picture his pursed lips, thin, like Jimmy's and the furrows between his eyes deepening. He cleared his throat, “Susan ...!”

“Yes dad.”

“Susan... I don’t think this...” He broke off, cleared his throat again, then asked. “Have you seen your mother?”

“No, not yet, I wanted to talk to you first.”

“Your mothe ...” He stopped. Susan could hear the rustling of papers in the background. “Your mother ...” He began again, his voice suddenly fainter, as if he had taken the phone away from his mouth. “Susan... I can’t talk to you just no ... I’m in the middle of something. ”

Again the uneasy silence.

Susan wanted to ask him if she could call and see him in his office. She was formulating the words when she heard the click as her father hung up. She stood listening to the disengaged brrr in her ear. A wave of rage surged up in her. She slammed the receiver down again and again, sending splinters of plastic flying around the booth. “Damn you. Damn you. Damn you,” she screamed, barging out and running blindly, cursing him.

When finally the flow of rage ebbed out of her, Susan found herself wandering on the foreshore. The last sliver of light was slipping from the sky and the first stars twinkled limply over the bay. She sat on the rocks, vacantly watching them come to life, her thoughts racing ahead of her across the darkening water.

How long she sat there she was not aware, debating within herself as to whether she had done the right thing coming back. Was it already too late? Had anything really changed? With Jimmy? Her father? Her mother? With herself? Had she held on to her anger too long? Why the hell hadn’t she contacted them sooner, she berated herself. Why hadn’t she, at least, sent a card to warn them she was on her way?

But, she remembered, they were not all bad times. The tide had turned and the sea smells and the swish of the receding waves on the darkened foreshore brought back memories of swimming and picnicking and sailing on the bay, throwing out bait for pollock and mackerel. It seemed such a long time ago.

Finally, cold and weary, she headed into town to the Old Haunt, the public house she had frequented with her friends before she left.

When she entered the bar of the 'Haunt' she was stopped in her tracks by the bright lights and the glitzy newness of it. It was packed with people she didn't recognize and even the bar staff were strangers to her. But it was warm and lively and that was what she needed right now. As she pushed her way to the counter she felt a hand on her shoulder.

"Susie. Hey, Susie?"

She turned. The voice was familiar but she didn't recognize the face.

"Steve," the face said grinning. "You haven't forgotten me surely ...?"

"Stevie." Susan laughed and pointed to his hair. "What happened to you?"

The last time she had seen Steve his long hair was parted in the centre and hung, tangled, over his shoulders, a straggly hippy-style mustache dangling either side of his mouth. Now, he had a short-back-and-sides hair cut, with a neat little fuzz over his top lip, and wearing a shirt and tie.

Susan giggled. "You look like a bank manager. What happened?"

"I'm gone respectable." Steve laughed, waving his empty glass over the heads of the crowd at the bar man. "Will I call you one, Susie?"

"Just a coke."

"You serious?" His eyebrows shot up in surprise. Susan, he remembered, had been able to knock back the pints better than any of them in the old days, but he let it go and ordered.

They found some seats in a corner and squeezed in. Steve explained about his hair cut. It was Susan's ex-boyfriend *'Animal'* Hayes' fault, he told her, grinning. He had been the singer and songwriter in Steve's band. "He got an offer from a group that was going to Berlin and left us." He snapped his fingers. "Just like that! There was murder when he split. But you know the *'Animal'*, when he made up his mind he did just what he liked. So he went and the band fell apart." Steve laughed. "I couldn't get another singer who could write so I got a job selling word processors instead. I just play the odd pub gig now. Can't imagine why you hung around with him, he was a wild man, but you got sense in the end."

"I wonder," Susan muttered then asked about the rest of the gang.

Steve told her how they had dispersed after the band broke up. The band had been their fulcrum. "It wasn't the same any more," he said. "You're just as well out of it." He talked on, ordering more rounds, but Susan was tired now and wanted to go home. Steve said he'd walk that way with her. When they got to the flat it was in darkness. Jimmy was already in bed. Susan invited Steve in for a coffee, warning him to be quiet, explaining that Jimmy would throw a fit if they woke him. He had always detested her 'rock and roll' friends.

While they were drinking their coffee Susan told Steve how she had worked as a volunteer in the drop-in centers in London, living on the dole, and making extra cash collecting glasses in Irish pubs, eventually becoming full time on a government scheme as Crèche trainee assistant, at a women's' centre. "It was watching all those unfortunate kids, every day," she said, smiling wistfully, "that started me thinking and got me off the drink. Then I began to write."

Stephen's eyebrows shot up in surprise. "I didn't know you had a touch of the bard in you," he grinned.

"It was mostly trying to explain to myself what had gone wrong at home," she told him. "Why my father kept pushing me to take a degree when I had no interest in it and why my mother drank so much. I was trying to sort out why I felt like a misfit in my own family. Writing it all down helped, like keeping a diary, but after the event. I began to get it out of my system, and see it all from a distance. Then the writing became poems."

Steve watched the growing excitement on Susan's face as she talked, her eyes widening as though she was standing on a white capped mountain, surveying a world of promise stretched out like a coloured tapestry before her.

“After a while I went to a women’s writing group,” she continued eagerly. “I was scared at first and just sat and listened. But I could see they were all as scared as me. They encouraged me to read some of my poems. It was amazing. I realized we were all telling the same story. After that I read there every week. They told me they were putting a book together, something from everyone in the group, and that I should submit a few of my poems. I was unsure at first. The poems were too personal, all about my dad and mam, and me caught somewhere in the middle. But they said, ‘Look, we’re all in the same boat, luv’. So I did. Three poems. The book is coming out in two weeks time. I have to be back for that.”

“Hey, listen.” Steve sat up enthusiastically. “Have you any of them with you. Maybe I could put them to music. I could get a new band together. Do your poems like The Doors did Morrisons.”

Susan shook her head, laughing at his childlike eagerness. “They don’t work like that. No rhymes”.

Steve laughed too. “Yeah. I know what you mean. I was only joking. But I’d love to hear one of them?”

Susan was thoughtful for a moment, staring into her coffee cup; a deep well. “This is a new one,” she said and began to recite softly.

“Endlessly, endless, the night is cold

The stars sail by my will

I watch them go

And trace their cobwebbed patterns with my nail

On breathy daybreak windows.

Whispfully, whispful, the cobweb breaks

Into rivulets of dew

The roseroot for her breakfast takes.

Carefully, careful, the rose awakes

And pouts her lips to the sun

And drinks the dew.

I saw her.

It froze upon my mind.

Endlessly, endless."

When she finished they sat in hushed silence for a number of minutes. Susan, with head bowed, eyes closed, and tears on her cheeks. Steve pictured her, sitting at some lonely London bed-sit window, staring out at the world, trying to make some sense of it all. He put his arm around her, comfortingly, and drawing her close, kissed her gently.

"Jesus Susie," he breathed softly, caressing her ear with his lips, "that was beautiful."

. . .

When Jimmy stumbled over them the next morning, wrapped together on the floor in Susan's sleeping bag, he flew into a rage and threw them out.

Susan found Julie, working in the same boutique as when she had last seen her. Although Susan had not shared an intimate friendship with any woman, even at collage, Julie had been the closest to her among the band's followers. Even though Susan thought her somewhat flappish at times, behind all her theatrics, she was a sound friend.

Julie shrieked and abandoned the customer she was serving when she spotted Susan standing with her rucksack in the doorway of the shop She threw herself on Susan and hugged her warmly.

"Welcome back. Welcome back," she shrieked, stepping back and holding Susan at arms length, scrutinizing her with the pinched face of an irate school teacher before bursting into laughter. "You're a bitch, Susie, a right bitch. Disappearing like that! Not even a card! But here you are ... and it's so good to have you back." She called over her shoulder to the other assistant, that she was taking her morning break early, as she pulled Susan outside by the arm.

Over coffee Julie quizzed Susan about London, saying how she wished she had the courage to 'flee' herself. But, she lamented, she had her job, and a new boyfriend who wanted to marry her and buy a house, and on top of it all her poor mother was ailing. How could she get away ...?

Susan was highly amused at the way Julie jingled her bondage chains like an arm-full of bracelets. You'll never change, she thought, and tried explaining how London was not the paradise Julie thought it to be. "It's big, glamorous and exciting, at first," she said. "Oh yes. But at the same time, it can swallow you up."

"But you've made such a go of it, Susie," Julie exclaimed, ignoring Susan's serious face, and grasping her hand across the table. "Your book and everything! And you seem so ... so sure of yourself.

Susan shook her head wryly at Julie's theatrical antics and explained that it had not been her choice. "Do you honestly think I would have gone there if it hadn't been for what happened at home," she asked. "I wish I could just come back and live an ordinary life here. It's crazy over there. Mad."

"Oh, Susie, do come back," Julie cried, her heavily mascaraed eyelashes flapping. "You can move in with me. I could get rid of my present flat mate. I'm not overjoyed with her anyway. She's stopped working and just mopes around all day. She's driving me crazy. Her name's Carol but she calls herself Karl – with a K. I think she's a... a... y'know." Julie made a face.

Susan laughed. "A lesbian?"

Julie flicked her eyes around the cafe in case there was anyone she knew. "Shhh!"

Susan laughed again at her antics.

Julie hurried on. "But we'd have great times together Susie!" She clapped her hands like an excited child then checked her watch. "Oh hell, I have to get back to the shop," she pouted, handing Susan a spare key and directions to her new flat, warning her to be sure and be back for dinner at eight. She wanted to hear all about London, "And I mean everything," she insisted before she ran off.

Susan went to drop off her rucksack. There was no sign of Julie's flat mate. It was a spacious flat in a new apartment block that had not been built when Susan had left. It smelled of fresh paint and was bright and airy with large picture windows giving a pleasant view of the river. It was the extreme opposite to the 'squats' she had shared in London. Julie roughing it? Not in a million years, Susan chuckled to herself, watching the river tumbling past below. She decided to go and confront her father. It was now or never.

Arriving at the university she headed straight for her father's office. But it was not where she remembered. The Porter directed her to a new wing. It seemed, Susan thought, that they had waited for her to leave before rebuilding the city.

When she finally stood outside her father's new office, her earlier resolve to storm right in and confront him face-to-face failed her. She stood, frozen with indecisiveness, staring at his nameplate, Professor Seamus T. Scannell, Department of Philosophy, reading the words over and over again as if caught in a time block.

His voice drifted to her from behind the door. She leaned closer and listened. He appeared to be dictating lecture notes, his disembodied voice drowning on and on. Susan caught some of the words and recognized passages form Sartre on Responsibility and Duty. Anger welled up in her at the irony of these words spilling so easily from his mouth. Then there was a crash and a voice shouting, Hypocrite! In the same shocking instant, she recognized it as her own voice and her own fist pounding on the door. The sound of her father's dictation ceased abruptly and the thud of a chair being knocked back came to her through the door. But before it was flung open, Susan, unnerved by her own emotional outburst, had fled from the building.

Angry and disheartened, she spent the remainder of the afternoon wandering about town, filling in time, looking at the numerous changes that had taken place in her absence. She met a few people she knew and sat drinking coffee and chatting for a while. But she was bored explaining again and again what she had been doing away and went back to Julie's flat to wait until dinner.

Julie's flat mate eyed her coldly when she arrived. Susan saw a small woman, in her early thirties, with large intense eyes staring out of what, she thought, could have been a pretty face if the woman would try smiling. Baggy jeans and sweater gave her the appearance of trying to hide inside an old sack. She introduced herself, 'Karl with a K', and said nothing more.

Susan explained who she was and that she might be staying for a few days. Karl shrugged noncommittally and sat on the couch fumbling with tobacco and papers, making a cigarette, finally offering the packet to her. Susan rolled hers deftly, causing Karl to stare, before they lit up and sat smoking on opposite ends of the couch in silence.

Susan closed her eyes and tried to relax, not wanting to think. From time to time she could feel Karl's eyes on her. She seems positively wired up, Susan thought, and imagined that any conversation with her would not be a light one. She had encountered many like her in the drop-in centre and supposed that she had probably been like that herself at the beginning. But at this moment she was too concerned with her own thoughts to get involved in any problems this woman might have.

"You English?" Karl asked suddenly.

Surprised at the question, Susan turned to face her. Karl's eyes bored into hers, the expression on her face crossed between hostility and awe. "English?" Susan retorted. "No. Why?"

"Uhh," Karl grunted. "Thought you were. You sound a bit."

"I've lived there for a while," Susan said, "that's all."

"Uhh." Karl shrugged. "London?"

"Yes."

"What's it like?"

"It's all right." Susan took a drag on her cigarette. "Why?"

"Just wondered." Karl busied herself rolling another cigarette. "Might go over sometime."

Susan checked her watch. It was now half past six and Julie would be home soon from work. Karl was getting on her nerves. She wondered what it would be like to sit between her and Julie at dinner? Karl was balled up in her corner of the couch pulling nervously on cigarette after cigarette, filling the room with smoke, and showing no sign of doing anything about preparing dinner.

Susan couldn't take it any longer and, rising to leave, asked her to apologize to Julie, saying she had something urgent to do.

. . .

When Susan arrived outside the house in which she had spent twenty years growing up, the familiarity of its red bricked front, with the white painted door and windows, tugged at her heart. The brightly lit rooms on the ground floor glowed like a welcoming beacon in the night. Her mother's rose bushes, standing stiffly in the stillness, seemed to be guarding the trim green lawn. The low wall surrounding it all appeared to hold everything together in its embrace.

A passionate desire to be a part of it again, even under these strained circumstances, urged Susan to run straight to the front door. But the terror of further reproach held her back.

A car swung around the corner of the street catching her in a beam of headlights. Susan turned away quickly to avoid recognition. The car passed on. It was only then she realized her father's car was not parked in the driveway. What day is it, she wondered. Wednesday? Didn't her father always have meetings on Wednesday nights? She was almost certain he had. Her father was a punctilious man and, if he wasn't home by now, it meant he was still working. She brightened. This would give her the chance to speak to her mother alone.

At that instant, she heard the front door open and a woman emerged from the brightly lit hallway. Susan's heart faltered with a pang of love mingled with dread, as the older woman wrapping a cardigan tightly around her against the cooler night air, took a few steps forward and, looking up, caught sight of her. Her mother stopped dead, startled, as if seeing a phantom.

"Susan? Is that you Susan?" she called out tentatively, peering at the apparition, her voice echoing hollow in the stillness. Susan, frozen on the spot, wrestled between excitement and confusion, not knowing which way to go.

"Susan!" Her mother's voice rose sharply, vexed at this ghost who would not identify itself.

Susan, cowed by the woman's shrill tone, took a hesitant step forward. "Hello Mam," she mumbled,

"I was coming out to close the gate," her mother began to explain, her voice keenly under control again. "I thought it was you. So you've condescended to pay us a visit?"

Susan closed the gate behind her and stood with her back to it almost afraid to go any further. They stood only feet apart gazing at each other. She had expected her mother to look much older but there was hardly any change at all. If anything, she looked healthier now than when she had last seen her. She's stopped drinking, Susan though hopefully.

Her mother's eyes, green, like her own and wide, with a slight upward slant at the edges, even in the dusky light seemed sharper than she remembered, but there was a raw austerity in them that made her wary.

"Well," her mother said, pragmatically, as if simply stating a fact, "I knew you'd be back someday," and, turning abruptly, led the way into the house. "Have you eaten?" her mother asked when they were in the kitchen. "I've finished dinner but I can make you something. A sandwich?" Taking Susan's bewildered nod as acceptance and, pointing to a chair, commanding her prodigal daughter to sit, she turned and busied herself at the work top, preparing the sandwich in silence.

Susan sat nervously barely daring to breathe. She had never expected to be sitting in this kitchen, at this table, ever again. It was unreal after all this time. So familiar and yet so removed. And what of her mother's attitude? Susan had expected, even hoped for, accusations, tears, hysterics, she didn't know what. But this cool indifference chilled her. As if Susan had only stayed out over night and drawn upon herself her mother's chagrin, instead of the reality, that she had been a fugitive from her home for the past two years.

She watched her mother's straight back as she worked. The wide shoulders and hips were more pronounced now; the waist somewhat thicker; the hair shorter but still black as a raven's. Is this what I'll look like when I'm her age Susan wondered. A sudden rush of love welled up in her for this older woman who had given her life. Oh God, she cried silently, why didn't I run to her and throw my arms around her.

Her mother finished making the sandwich, wet the tea, and distributed cups, saucers, teapot, sugar and milk on the table without a word. The practiced ritual of a thousand meals served. She placed the sandwich in front of Susan and sat opposite.

"Eat," she said. The single word a command.

Susan could only pick at the sandwich; her hunger had suddenly evaporated.

"So", her mother began. "Is this a flying visit, or ..." She stopped, distracted for a moment, then asked bluntly, "You're not pregnant ...?"

Susan started. "No."

"Hmmm." Her mother considered her for a minute. "And when did you arrive? Today?"

"Yesterday," Susan replied, cowed by her mother's brusque tone. "I stayed with Jimmy."

"And how is James, I haven't seen him for a while." She picked up the teapot and held it, poised, over Susan's cup. "Still studying hard, I suppose," she continued, as if talking to herself. The teapot hovered. "Going to be like his father. Head stuck in books all his life."

Her mother stared at the teapot as though she had momentarily forgotten its function, then, replacing it carefully on its mat without pouring she began to trace the pattern on the table top with her finger, ignoring her daughter. Perhaps I was wrong, Susan thought, she has been drinking. She waited for the calm to break; for her mother to throw something, a cup, a tantrum, even herself, across the kitchen. But nothing.

The finger stopped tracing and her mother looked up as if surprised to find Susan there. "So what have you been doing with yourself," she asked. But her tone held little concern.

Susan explained. Her mother listened without comment, a vacant expression like a veil shading her face. Susan felt as if she was talking to herself and hurried to get it over with.

"You seem to have carved a little niche for yourself right enough," her mother commented when she finished. "There's hope for us all," she continued, picking up the teapot again.

"I rang dad yesterday. Did he not tell you?" Susan asked.

The hand, holding the teapot, jerked suddenly, crashing against the cup knocking it awry.

"No... !" Her mother retorted, hastily straightening the cup and saucer and beginning to pour the tea again, "... he didn't." She looked up sternly at her daughter, her eyes ablaze.

Susan fidgeted with her uneaten sandwich afraid to return her mother's look. "He couldn't talk to me," she stammered. "I don't know - wouldn't talk - he was at a meeting or something. We got cut off. I think. It sounded like it."

"Hah!." Her mother laughed; a single explosion, making Susan jump. "Hung up on you? *Hah!*" Her voice rose sharply, sarcasm smeared across her mouth like crooked lipstick. She gave the table a resounding whack with the flat of her hand rattling the crockery. "Did he now ... *Hah!*"

She's mad, Susan thought, horrified. The drink has finally done this.

The older woman glared at her daughter across the table. She wiped a hand quickly over her mouth several times as if to make sure the lunacy didn't erupt again. "You may as well know," she continued, her voice hollow with bitterness, "you may as well know now, Susan, that he doesn't ... stay here any more. Your father and I ..." She took a deep breath. "All the men have left. Jimmy, as you know, has been gone since he started college. I never see him. And now ... since you ...” She stopped abruptly and laid her hands flat on the table, leaning heavily on them until the veins stood out, as though attempting to squash the unfinished sentence beneath them.

“There’s just...” she stopped, studying the backs of her hands before continuing, “... and this old house. This is what you’ve come back to.”

Susan mumbled. “I’m sorry.”

Her mother gave a feeble laugh. “You have nothing to be sorry about,” she said, pushing herself up, and, leaning over, she rested her hand lightly on her daughter’s shoulder for a second, like a cold kiss, before going out of the kitchen.

“Oh God,” Susan screamed inwardly as she listened to her mother laboriously climbing the stairs like a crushed widow; the creaking floorboards overhead; doors opening and closing on empty rooms. What the hell is she up to? she wondered. Is each step, each sound, calculated to prick me with its accusing finger. All this emptiness. My bloody fault!

Her thoughts scrambled around in her head. Even when she was away, writing her stories, her poems, trying to understand what had happened, it was still going on. The arguments. The scenes. Her father packing; storming out. Jimmy taking sides; not visiting anymore. Her mother left alone to face the disgrace of the bleak deserted house.

And Jimmy! Susan’s temper flamed. The bastard! The least he could have done was warn me. Not let me walk into this trap blindfolded. This is a thin slice of his punishment for me.

When her mother returned to the kitchen and sat opposite Susan again it was as if a cold black vapour had seeped into every crevice of the room; every pore of her skin. What was all that banging around upstairs about? Susan wanted to challenge her. But she could not bear to look into her mother's eyes, fearful of what she might see.

“So now you know,” she heard the low, sardonic voice, accuse,

"…this is what you've done to us."

She was trapped. Afraid to look the demon in the face. Scared to run but more terrified of what would happen if she stayed. She had to get out. But how do you escape the woman turned fiend. Where can you hide from the mother turned monster? You cannot. There is no place. She runs in your bloodstream. What did you think you could change by coming back? Nothing. It only gets worse; more bizarre, more complicated.

"It's not my fault," she cried out, fighting back tears of frustration. "It's not ... it's not."

"SUSAN!" the monster snapped.

"No. It's not fair. It's not fair." She jumped up, knocking her chair back and glared angrily at ... this... But it was no monster, no unearthly creature, sitting, arms folded, leaning on the table opposite, an abstracted expression glazing the cat-like eyes. No. It was only an old, booze-jaded, woman.

Yes, the woman who had brought her into this world. Yes, her mother, but cloaked in the guise of a bogus lunatic indulging in absurd mind games with her. "It's not my fault," Susan shrieked.

"Sit down," her mother commanded. "Shouting will get you nowhere,"

Susan stormed away, turned back, twisted away again, like a caged animal. Her mother's eyes stalked her, a storm cloud gathering in her face.

"Sit down, Susan."

Susan stood, wrestling within herself. Which way to go?

"SIT DOWN," her mother snapped and rapped the table with her finger.

Susan stiffened. Fumbled in her bag for a cigarette. Lit it. Looked around for an ashtray. There was none. She blew a puff of smoke at the ceiling, then scraped her chair to the table and sat.

"Now," her mother said, rearranging the delft on the table, "this is how we stand." She pointed to the individual pieces. "The teapot - me. The plate - your father. The saucer - Jimmy. The knife - You." She laid them in a square, like a bizarre chess game waiting for the final moves of play. "At least we all know, now, where we stand. There's no illusions anymore."

Susan watched the ridiculous charade with mounting disgust. Mad, she thought. This woman is out of her mind.

Suddenly her mother sighed deeply. Her whole body slumped for a beat, then checked itself, straightening again. She rose abruptly and cleared all the delft off the table into the sink with a clatter and turning her back on it gripped the top of the chair tightly, so that her knuckles shone white in the stark fluorescent light. She surveyed the empty table-top - the battle ground - now cleared, between them before speaking.

"I'm sick of it," she said. "I want no more of it. I'm too tired. I'm going up to bed. Come back tomorrow, or whenever ... I'm not going anywhere." She walked out stiffly. "Put out the light when you're leaving, or leave it on, it's all the same," she said and, once again, with heavy steps, climbed the stairs.

Susan sat motionless, listening to her mother moving about, above her head, preparing for bed. She waited, hoping she might come down again, wondering if she should go up and ... and what? What more was there to say? Gradually the sounds from upstairs ceased.

She finished her cigarette, brushed the fallen ash from the table and stood up. There was a cold, hollowed-out feeling inside her, as if all her natural responses - to fight, to argue, to scream, lash out, cry, forgive, reconcile - were extinct.

She took a saucer from the pile in the sink and stubbed out the cigarette. An old urge to wash the dishes and tidy up, surfaced, but she shook it off. Why bother? Confused, she sat down again and lit another cigarette, staring blankly at the lines of grain running along the table. Left to right. Right to left. Light and dark. Running parallel. Separating each side of the knots. Running on again. Disappearing over the edge, only to reappear once more on the other side. Going round in circles. Just like me, she thought sardonically.

If my friends in the writing group could only see me now, Susan thought, ironically.

They had urged her to return and make peace with her family while awaiting the publication of their book. One woman in particular, Mary-Anne, a fellow expatriate in her fifties, implored her in the name of God to go now, before it was too late. "I put it off and put it off," Mary-Anne had sobbed, shaking her grey head at her own stupidity "Thirty years it is since. 'Tis too late now I'm afraid. Go now, don't be like me, *a girsha*, or you'll regret it for the rest of your life."

During the months of preparation for the book these women had become more than just a group of individuals telling their stories. Their common purpose and similar predicaments had united them in a sisterhood of friendship and understanding, so it was with confidence, bolstered by their support and encouragement, that Susan had set out. She remembered the longing in Mary-Anne's eyes. She could still hear the sad voice as she waved good-bye at Victoria station. "Do it for me, love. In the name o' God." She did not fully believe in Mary-Anne's God but she felt the older woman's plea to make amends before it was too late was simply common sense based on bitter experience. Susan did not want to end up like that, shriveled up in her own misery.

But now, having undergone her brother's hostility, the humiliation of her father's snub and her mother's hostile rejection, her courage began to evaporate and she wondered if anyone could ever undo this tangled knot.

Back at Julie's flat there was a note for her on the table. '*Gone to McGee's. Back lounge. Join us. Love, Julie.*'

Susan hadn't the strength to face them in their enforced mid-week alcoholic jollity after the encounter with her mother. She pulled her sleeping bag out of the rucksack with a weary sigh, spread it on the couch and stretched out. She needed to calm down, think, plan. But her thoughts would not settle, like a thousand stray beads, rattling around within the confines of a tin can - her head. Her mother! Her father! Her brother! She jumped up and threw on her jacket. Jimmy! Yes, she raged, he should have warned me!

The lights were on in Jimmy's flat. She still had his spare key and stormed in on him among his books. He was already on his feet, shoulders bunched, preparing to fend off the intruder.

"You. What the hell ..." he blurted.

"You bastard, Jimmy," she hissed, the momentum of her anger breaking through his defensive stance, attacking him with flailing fists. "You could have told me. At least warned me," she thundered, raining blows on his chest. "I've just been up to the house - Mam - the least you could have done was warned me. I suppose you think this is some kind of joke? Your little perverse game? You're a snake, Jimmy. A *slimebag* ..."

Jimmy pushed her away roughly, throwing her against the table, knocking books from their neat piles. "Nobody asked you to come back," he barked, eying her warily as he bent to retrieve the books that had tumbled to the floor. "I told you. You can't change anything. It's done."

"That's not what I mean," Susan stormed, fighting back tears of rage, watching him rearrange his precious books "I walked in there. I didn't know anything. Some brother you are. You're a bastard Jimmy."

Jimmy stopped abruptly and stood for a moment in silence glaring at his sister. He pointed first to her then to himself, a leer spreading across his thin lips. "I'm a bastard ..." he said, nodding his head in mock assertion, "... that's a good one." He replaced the text book he was holding carefully on its stack and dropped into his chair, leaning back, all the time keeping his eyes on Susan's angry face. "That's good," he repeated and began to snigger, "I'm a bastard."

"So what would you call yourself?" Susan demanded. "A friend? A brother? What?"

"Call it what you like," he replied, fussing with his books again, methodically aligning their spines on top of each other, "but I can assure you I'm not the bastard in this family. You've been to see your mother. You should know."

"I should know? Know what?" She felt like springing on him and smashing his jeering face on the table. Just like mam, she thought, another bloody game player. What is wrong with these people? "What dumb game are you playing now?" she demanded.

"No game."

"Then what..?"

Jimmy pursed his lips and ruminated for a minute before answering. His deliberating slowness was exasperating Susan's last reserve of self-restraint. When he did speak, it was as if each word was a poisoned dart aimed at the very depths of her soul. "What - you - are," he said.

Susan trembled with disbelief. "What ... ?"

Jimmy retreated behind his barricade of books. "You heard me," he said.

What you are. Susan's heart froze. What you are. The words rebounded around and around in her head. No, it couldn't be true, this was another of his cowardly warped pranks. I'll kill him! She took a step forward. The floor seemed to tilt under her feet. She faltered. Righted herself. Then turned in agony and stormed out into the night screaming.

"You're a liar, Jimmy. A damned liar."

. . .

When Susan awoke the following morning she felt as if shards of glass were being plunged through the back of her head piercing her eyes. She squeezed the heels of her hands into her eye sockets in a vein attempt to push back the pain.

The events of the previous night throbbed in her memory. The fight with Jimmy. Stumbling into the back lounge of McGees. No recollection of how she got there. Backslapping and welcoming cheers and drinks thrust into her hand. Smoke and heat and grinning faces behind endless pint glasses of black Guinness. Then somebody's flat. Loud, raucous music, and the spongy taste of hash on the back of her throat. Then blank.

Where was she? She sat up. A sheering blade of pain cut through her eyes and checked her halfway to her feet. She fell back on the couch. Whose couch? She sunk her head into her hands. Oh, yes. Remembering. Julie's Her stomach heaved but she was afraid to move.

"Hi."

The unexpected and unfamiliar voice in the darkened room startled her. Who was it? A shadowy figure moved to one side of her and a swish of opening curtains let in a shaft of sunlight instantly blasting the room with light. Susan covered her eyes against the vicious glare.

"You okay?" the voice asked from behind. Susan could only manage a muffled groan in reply. Karl came around the couch and stood in front of her.

"Where's the bathroom?" Susan moaned, swallowing back the bile rising in her throat.

Karl pointed.

Susan heaved herself off the couch and ran weakly through the door indicated and instantly threw up. Never again, she reproached herself, between waves of nausea wrenching at her stomach.

Back in the couch, white faced and drained, and wondering how she had managed to get herself into this sorry state, she gladly accepted the aspirin and glass of water pushed into her hands.

"Good night, huh?" Karl asked with mock cheerfulness.

Susan wished this intruder on her misery would just go away and leave her in peace but she was thankful for the medicine. She nodded. "I suppose so."

"You were pretty shot when you came back last night."

"I don't remember."

Karl shrugged. "Yeah. You and Julie". She watched Susan in silence for a minute. She seemed to be pondering some question. Then she asked. "Who's Jimmy? Your boyfriend?"

Why can't she shut up, Susan thought, I don't want to know about last night. But the woman is only trying to be sociable, I suppose. "My brother. Why?"

A glimpse of a smile crossed Karl's face but she made no answer.

You should smile more often, it wouldn't hurt you, Susan thought, remembering the other woman's scowling face of the previous afternoon. It seemed like years ago.

"I've coffee on," Karl said at length and went out to the kitchen.

"Thanks. I'd love some."

Susan attempted to shake off her foul humour. The medicine was taking effect and the pressure in her head began to ease. What's this one so chirpy about this morning, she wondered. Is she attempting to chat me up? What the hell. She threw the thought from her. Karl came in with mugs of coffee and handed her one.

"What did I say about my brother?" Susan asked.

Karl measured several spoons of sugar into her coffee. "You kept shouting you wanted to kill him," she said.

Susan laughed. It hurt her throat. "Dead right too!," she said.

Karl smiled faintly and looked away into the depths of her coffee. "Julie said you might be coming back to stay," she said, becoming serious again.

Susan shook her head. "No way."

She closed her eyes and groaned deeply. She hadn't any more time for Karl's banter. She could see where it was heading. It wasn't the first time her stocky build, close hair cut and leather jacket had attracted older women, but it wasn't Susan's preference.

She had more urgent things to think about. Like Jimmy's contemptuous accusation thumping around in her brain. She shook her head in desperation. A futile attempt to dislodge the memory of his leering face and hateful words. How could she face her mother again? But she knew it had to be done. She had to face the woman for better or worse. She laughed wryly at her choice of words and sprang off the couch. This time she would ring first as a warning. Feeling more decisive now she would demand answers, good or bad, regardless of the outcome. Too much time, she felt, was being wasted on this emotional merry-go-round.

. . .

Entering the kitchen behind her mother, Susan was filled with the desire to permeate this house, with her new-found and broadened experiences. Coming to it, this time in daylight, she felt stronger. The urge to run upstairs and breathe the air of her old bedroom and look in presses and lie on familiar beds tugged at her.

She pictured her bicycle in the garden shed and wondered if it still worked. But now, confronting her mother again across the kitchen table, with what Jimmy had thrown at her crouching like a serpent in her brain, she was numbed. It was as if an inhibited stranger had taken over her body.

"Mam," she began awkwardly, when her mother placed coffee and biscuits on the table and sat down. "Mam, I'm not happy ..."

Her mother snorted faintly. "Who is?"

"I don't mean it like that." Susan winced. "What I mean is - about what happened - what *is* happening."

Her mother sipped her coffee without answer. This is ridiculous, Susan thought, it's not easy for me and she's not trying to help at all.

"What I want to say is - I'm confused," Susan continued, "about what happened and is still going on." The picture of her mother alienating the delft in a square the previous night and saying that this is how they stood confronted her memory. She spread out her hands in supplication to her mother. For God's sake, don't build a stone wall between us like this, her heart sobbed. "What can I do?" She pleaded.

For the first time the older woman looked her straight in the eye. "Leave well enough alone," she said.

"But - how?"

"Susan," her mother began, "what happened, happened. It's not your fault or my fault or anybody's fault. Go back to London, or wherever you want, and forget it. There were circumstances which are out of your hands and there's nothing you can do about it. "

Susan moaned inwardly. Couldn't her mother see that she was trying to offer some semblance of an apology. Faltering though it may be, if she was using the wrong words - damn - if only her mother would throw down the defenses. Suppressing her rising anger Susan asked, "Who's hands is it in then, Gods?"

"It may well be," her mother answered tonelessly .

Susan could not stand it any longer. Her perplexity at the wall of ice thrown up in her face by her family was becoming impregnable. She jumped up in exasperation and began pacing back and forth across the kitchen, like a caged animal, mustering her forces for a final assault.

"Mam," she said, struggling to keep calm, "when I came back I was prepared for a row. I expected a fight. Anything to clear the air. To try and make up." She took a deep breath. "Dad hung up on me. You refuse to talk to me. And last night I had a terrible row with Jimmy. He accused me of ..." She stopped pacing and faced her mother. Oh God! How can I say what he accused me of? Instead she asked, "What happened after I left?"

"I've already told you."

"No. That's not it at all. It's only part of it," Susan cried. She didn't want any of what had happened to be true any more. Didn't want her parents separated. Didn't want to be continually fighting with them or with Jimmy. But, 'didn't want,' wouldn't make what Jimmy had called her, disappear. She had to know the truth.

"Mam ..." Susan's voice almost failed her with the weight of the question she desperately needed an answer to. "What Jimmy said - he told me I was ... " She faltered. How could she say it? Not your child. Nor his sister. Not my father's daughter. What ...? But there was only one appropriate word and as it left her lips she strangled it, hoping for denial, "Am I ... a ... bastard." She watched her mother carefully for reaction. "Is it true? I have to know."

The older woman froze for a second, then slowly, like a snail retreating into its shell, shrunk her head into her shoulders. "Go away," she breathed, almost inaudibly, "leave well enough alone."

The kitchen clock dropped the seconds into the weighty stillness, each moment drawing out into minutes - hours, it seemed.

"For Christ's sake, Mam, answer me," Susan screamed. "I can't take any more of this!"

Her mother's head shot out. "Don't you dare talk to me like that." The words lashed across Susan's face like a whip. "Don't you ever."

The two women glared at each other across the kitchen and it was as though they were not feet apart, but miles. The older woman's face twitched, twisted, and, as her daughter watched in horror it seemed as if aeons of agony marched in spasms across its contorted surface. Then, reaching its peak, it paused, suspended for a second, before slowly crumpling and falling like a condemned building under the impact of the demolition hammer. Huge tears gathered in her mother's eyes, overflowed, and streamed down her face, splashing on the table between them. She slumped forward cradling her face in her hands. Then, without warning, Susan too, burst into tears. "Oh, Mam," she cried. "I'm sorry."

The sound of their sobbing filled every crevice in the room, wave upon wave, rising and falling, answering each other in a bizarre emotional duet.

When finally their tears subsided, they sat, subdued, as on a calm sea after a raging storm, in the aftermath of release. Their swollen eyes and tear streaked faces mirrored each other across the room. Susan's mother looked at her daughter and it was with a tenderness that Susan had not witnessed for a long time. Then, in a hushed voice, her mother began.

"Before your father and I got married," she began, "there was another man." She held up her hand quickly to stop the question forming on her daughter's lips. "No, his name doesn't matter now. He's long out of it, emigrated to Australia. I was in love with both of them." A slim smile plucked at the corners of her mouth at the memory. "Oh, you think these kind of things didn't happen in my day. Your father's friend was keen to marry me and start afresh in a new country. But I wasn't prepared to leave. I suppose that was what made up my mind for me so I married your father."

"So Jimmy was wrong," Susan exclaimed.

"Wait," her mother said. "No, it's not that simple. When I married, and may God forgive me, I was carrying you. I suppose with your father's friend leaving and me being pregnant, I was terrified, I rushed into it. Your father was a post-graduate, and at the time quite brilliant, a great future ahead of him. He didn't want any scandal so we were married." She stopped and considered her words before continuing. "The problem was, I wasn't sure whose child you were... well..." Her voice caught for a moment and she looked away. Then cleared her throat and continued. "I knew alright, every woman knows, but I didn't want to admit it..."

Susan opened her mouth to protest but her mother stopped her. "This is not easy for me," she said. "You wanted to know. Please."

"But surely," Susan pressed her, "surely you could have found out. You could've ..."

Her mother shook her head. "It wasn't as simple as that. Sometimes you don't want to know. Knowing would only complicate things. What if it turned out the way you didn't want it to be? Luckily, when you were born you resembled me, so there were no questions. To me it didn't matter, so it was best to leave 'well enough' alone.

"But as you grew up I could see your father watching you. For signs, or tendencies you might have, that would show him. He never said anything but I knew he was waiting. It broke my heart to watch him. You see, his friend, though he had the same qualifications as your father, was not as serious about life as him. He was a bit reckless. You could say he was a waster."

"What happened to him?"

Her mother sighed. "He took a position in a university, similar to your father's, in Australia. Unfortunately, he had a drink problem, let it get the better of him, got fired from his job. I don't know what happened after that - it was the last I heard of him."

Susan burst out. "So my... Father... my real Father is a waster somewhere in Australia... *Jesus!*"

" I didn't say that." Her mother snapped. She studied Susan's distraught face for a moment, then continued calmly. "It's a long time ago. It's 'water under the bridge'. Let it be child'.

Susan struggled to keep back her anger. Her mother sighed deeply and continued.

"Then James was born, and it was after that your father began to change. Oh, it happened gradually. It was as if we each had a child now. Jimmy was his and you were mine. It was ridiculous, all in his mind. It made no difference to me. You were both mine. But I watched him choosing and favouring - your father could be very subtle - I could do nothing to stop him. I began to hate him for it... "

She stopped and dabbed at her eyes.

"There were times when nobody would know it. It was like we would forget and just be like any other family. Of course there were good times. But gradually there weren't. Then, you went to college, and everything seemed to be fine for a while, until you started to hang around with that band and come home smelling of drink. You should have done like James, got out then, and got a flat. And then you started to miss lectures and wouldn't study..."

Susan hung her head.

"No," her mother said gently, "it wasn't your fault. But it was then your father began to point the finger and it became clear that he thought he had the final proof that he you were not his child. That you were just like his old friend. A waster. You would disgrace him, a professor with a growing reputation."

"But after all that time," Susan remonstrated, "that's ridiculous!"

"Your father is a very strange man." Her mother answered dolefully. "For all his brilliance and learning he's just as proud as the next - and as jealous. He wouldn't - no, couldn't, accept that any child of his would be a failure."

"So, in theory, according to him I was not his daughter," Susan said in disgust. "If I hadn't dropped out everything would have been okay. I can't believe this."

"Don't," her mother said softly, "don't blame yourself. It's not your fault. It's not anybody's fault. If he couldn't accept you as you were, regardless of whether you followed in his footsteps or not..." She shrugged, leaving the sentence hanging in the air.

Susan shook her head to try to clear the jumble of thoughts. "So my real Father... But why did you..." Susan began again uneasily, "But why did you push me out?"

Her mother gave a light dry laugh. "To protect you, child," she said. "To save you. You're like I used to be Susan, you kick and fight, but behind it all there's no badness in you. I knew you'd come back. And I prayed for the day. But when you did you frightened me. All this nonsense would be dragged up again. I didn't think I could cope with it." She stopped as tears began to blur her eyes once more.

Mother and daughter sat in deep thought for a number of minutes.

"That word," Susan's mother began again, "what James accused you of. It's the most hideous word in the English language - in any language. To accuse any child of that is barbaric. A child is simply a child. In the eyes of God all children are the same. Beautiful. Innocent. It is not a 'this' or a 'that'. But unfortunately some men ..." She left the sentence unfinished. "Your father is one of them. May God forgive him."

She joined her hands on the table in front of her, fingers entwined, head bowed, as if in prayer. "So now you know," she finished.

Susan's thoughts swarmed in her head, the relief and joy, frustration and pain, all seeking to be unraveled and understood; solutions found and a final resting place in this menagerie of doubt and confusion.

She gazed lovingly at the woman who had borne all their burdens and trials for the past twenty-five years and noticed for the first time the slump of her shoulders and threads of grey in her hair. Reaching out, with a renewed warmth in her heart, she placed her hand on her mother's and felt the silent love flow between them.

. . .

That afternoon Susan decided to return to London without delay. It would take more than a few rushed days, she knew, to achieve what she was now determined to do.

Before she left she sat to compose a careful letter to her father. Or the man she had called Father. It was a few minutes before she had the courage to begin with *'Dear Dad'.* Then continued

'I have had a long talk with Mam. She has explained everything to me. I realize what has happened is difficult to accept and has pushed us apart. I firmly believe that if we make an effort we can, at least, stop fighting and hating each other. I am not saying that I fully understand all the problems, or who is right or wrong. At this point I think it's irrelevant. But I think that we should make an effort to understand and come to terms with it.

I am returning to London today but will be back before the end of the month for good. I sincerely hope that we can talk then and find a way to clear up this mess we are in. That is my dearest wish.'

She thought long, pen posed above paper, before adding,

'All my love, your daughter, Susan'.

Then she made a copy to her brother. When she had addressed the envelopes and laid them in her shoulder bag a sliver of panic began to gnaw at the pit of her stomach. Would it make any difference? Will it only give them another chance to deride me, even more, for baring my soul? Just because I feel like starting over doesn't necessarily mean they will too. Perhaps they're already too entrenched in their defenses to even want to make a change. But I have to try. I must try. My future - *Our future* and happiness depends on it.

On her way to the bus station, Susan placed the letters in the post box with a determined prayer, and then prepared herself for the long journey home.

Jes sat in his tree. He called it 'his tree' ever since he was a boy when it was the largest thing in his life. This old majestic ash, with lined and fissured bark and pale green cigar shaped leaves, was, his father told him, a 'mother tree'. The tree became a sanctuary where he spent happy hours among the leafy embrace of its branches. For him it was a playground in the sky.

When he was a child, this ancient tree, stood, dignified, over hundreds of acres of farmland. Now it seemed to gaze despairingly at the housing estates surrounding it as though threatening to creep up on its roots and smother it.

Jes felt the same despair. He traced the regimented lines of houses below him. When the tip of his finger came to a particular house he stopped. This was where *'Mother'* lived. He loathed the gross middle aged woman, who was destroying the life of Emma, his girlfriend, with her noxious sachets of snow-white powder. A deadly substance that spilled over his own life and that of his son.

Jes had courted Emma under this same tree. Their first kiss, with her back pressed up against its solid old trunk, was magical. This tree knew all their love secrets. This tree harbored in its sap the knowledge of the first time he had felt her soft warm flesh under her summer dress. Only five glorious summers ago.

The kids from the housing estate had given them a hard time that evening. They circled around, chanting, *'Jes's kissin' Em-ma, Jes's kissin' Em-ma',* pulling faces, giggling, and pointing pink tongues at them.

Had he the power to command the tree to lift one of it's giant roots out of the ground and stamp on them, Jes would have. Instead he only roared at them, *'Get lost ya little snots...!'* But of course they didn't. They were looking for a chase, but Jes was not prepared to give them one, because he was about to reach the pinnacle of his own pleasure. He wanted it to happen here in the embrace of this tree. This was the place: his most favorite place in the whole world. He wished he could carry Emma up into its sheltering coolness - to have made love to her for the first time along that strong wide branch - Aah, ecstasy !

When he returned home, Emma was sitting at the dressing table fixing her face. Not that she needed to do anything with it. Make-up only rendered her already fine features more pronounced.

Jes sat on the bed, watching, as she studied herself in the mirror. She pulled her perfect skin this way and that, searching for a possible flaw to be squeezed or covered or tended to. She needn't have bothered. But she continued anyway. Jes normally enjoyed the intimacy of the ritual. But neither of them were taking any pleasure in it today.

Emma eyed his serious face in the mirror. "What's wrong with you?" she snapped.

He shrugged. "Nothing."

She continued to search her face. Jes fidgeted and looked away.

"The trouble with you is," she said, teasing an imaginary pimple, her voice contorted by her manipulations, "you left home, in the physical. But not in the mental. Y'know. Your body left ... but not your mind ..."

Emma had been saying meaningless things like that, for the past nine months, ever since their son was born. It made no sense to Jes. He had been reared in this house, still lived here, and had never left home. He let the remarks go. Emma and the baby were his life. What really worried him was the continuing visits of *'Mother'* to his home. He despaired at their association.

"It's not an addiction!" Emma would scream at him. "I'm under control. It's as harmless as food or drink if it's taken in moderation. There's thousands of people doing it who live to a ripe old age, no bother. Too much of anything can kill you. Air. Water. Food." She'd eye him angrily while digging at his own weakness. "Drink! And you should know something about that! Don't you worry your sweet little head about me. It's all under control. *She* sees to that."

How could she be that naive? Jes knew there were exceptions to every rule, but in this case, the exceptions were of no importance to him. No amount of arguments or statistics could make her see the danger. Her mind was clouded to everything but her own misguided desires.

"You don't own me, y'know," she'd say. "I am ... what I am."

But he loved her so much he could deny her nothing. Not even this slow decline in her life. He hoped and prayed that, given time, he could convince her to stop before it was too late.

Jes slipped a tape into the ghetto blaster. But he couldn't concentrate, his mind was distracted by dark thoughts. He snapped it off again.

Emma turned from the mirror. "What's eating you?" she asked. "You're useless this last few months ever since you went on the dry."

For this kind of statement Jes had no counter-argument. Emma accusing him of changing ever since the baby arrived; since he gave up drinking. Could she not see that it was her drug-induced moods that dictated his behavior? Life had indeed changed drastically. In one way it was improved beyond measure with the birth of their son and, in another, it plummeted with Emma's addiction. Jes loves the baby. He loves her. But he hates what her habit is doing to them.

Emma turned back to the mirror. "Look, I've got someone coming - go sit in your tree for a while."

He knew who she meant but played the game for what little it was worth.

"Who ...?" he asked.

Emma pulled a face at his reflection.

"Ah, for fuck sake," Jes growled, twisting with annoyance. Storming from the room, he ran down the stairs, slamming the door behind him.

. . .

Alone in his tree perch, his thoughts crowded with demons, Jes watches as '*Mother'* arrives.

The Bitch! The Witch! The Ball of Slime! Not my mother. Not Emma's mother. She's the mother to all her little vein-shooters. And they are all her children. She feeds their wasted dreams. Grants their perverted wishes. Succors them to come unto her. And when they are no more ... Aah. *'Mother'* knows best. There will always be more ...

Jes visualizes the scene now taking place in the house. *'Mother'* sits on a straight-backed chair. She slumps, fat and lumpy, inside her rabid fur coat. Tarnished and musty, make-up smudged on her face, she chain-smokes like an old man. Jes cannot believe she was ever young, he sees her as born already ancient.

Speaking is a great effort for her. She croaks through the wall of nicotine lodged in her wind-pipe. Yet below the gravelly tone sneaks a resonance of old gentility.

"You all right...?"

Emma, her youthful beauty increased a millionfold in the presence of this decrepitude, shrugs. "Yeah. I'm okay."

"And himself...?"

Emma shrugs again.

"Treating you all right ...?" *'Mother'* asks, as any mother might.

The slim shoulders lift - then fall.

"Hmmm ..." *'Mother'* muses, "you look a bit thin."

"I'm all right."

The older woman bares a cigarette-stained smile. "Call me *Mother* ... You'll feel better."

When her drug addicted 'children' finally get around to calling her *'Mother'* she knows they're hooked. Hooked to her and to her costly merchandise.

"And the little one?"

"Fine ..." Emma swallows hard, struggling to say the next word.

"... *Mother*".

The old woman nods. Just once. Satisfaction in her rheumy eyes.

"That's good."

She reaches tentacled fingers into a small snake-skin handbag and places the plastic package of forbidden dreams on Emma's coffee table. Heaving her bulk off the chair she wraps the fur around her. Mission completed.

"You're a little behind," she wheezes, pursing the crooked smear of lip-stick that she calls a mouth. "But we can fix that little matter up later."

Catching her own reflection in the mirror, she turns away quickly as though she has seen something unsettling. Her yellow eyes survey the room's tidiness. "You keep the place nice. That's good. I won't hold you. I'll be off."

She exits the sitting room as she entered - a rolling barrel of rot - shuffling slowly down the hall.

. . .

A scene plays in Jes's mind.

A man on a park bench offers Emma a cigarette,

"A great invention - cigarettes," he says, twisting his thin lips into a smile. "Introduction like. Starts the ball rolling. A way of getting over those initial barriers. Have one."

Emma doesn't want any of it. Not him nor his conversation starters. She shrugs him off and walks away. Mister Cigarette hurries after her.

The kids come running up and around him blocking his progress.

"*Giz a penny, mister. Giz a penny, mister. Ah, go on. Giz a penny mister.*"

He shoos them away, flapping his overcoat like skinny wings. They stalk him, and when he flicks his half-smoked cigarette away, lunge on it like trainee vultures. The boy reaches it first and grabs a pull before it goes out.

The little girl hops around taunting him. "*Am tellin'. Am tellin'. You wur smokin'. You wur smokin'.*"

She chases after him as he runs away puffing and blowing like a toy train.

'Mother Slimebag-of-Ecstasy', shuffling past, on her way to the next appointment, wheezes at them, mimicking their gutter accents.

"Shut up, youz! Go home to youzer mothers."

Noisy kids. She hates them. But she's not their *'Mother'* yet, so they have the right to ignore her - for the moment.

Spotting Jes up in his tree, she pauses and cranes her neck to stare at him, like a cat tunnel-visioning a bird. "You should've more sense ... You," she snarls.

Jes doesn't give her the satisfaction of a glance. "Fuckin' leach," he mutters under his breath, not wanting to insult the spirit of the tree by shouting it out loud.

. . .

Emma sprawls on the bed, her hands conjuring shapes in the air.

"Oh, my love," she moans. "My beautiful love prince. Come to me. Rescue your princess." She giggles. Images float before her in a thin-air play.

Jes watches her charade from the doorway. his face set with disgust.

Emma continues to play, mindless of him. "Take me through the ages. My prince. My knight. Ride with me on the winds." She giggles uncontrollably at her own silly romanticizing and reaches out her arms as though welcoming a lover. "Oh my love! My love."

Jes is at the bedside in two strides. He pulls her up by the arm and slaps her hard across the face. She falls back, limply, laughing hysterically. The baby cries out in the next room.

Jes hovers, undecided, glaring down at Emma. He leaves the room and returns cuddling the baby. Emma watches them with a glazed look on her face. Then, in a flash, she is off the bed attacking him.

"Give me my baby!"

Jes tries to side-step past, but she tears at him furiously. "GIVE ME MY BABY," she screams.

Fearful of the child coming to harm in the tussle Jes hands him over.

The baby is howling, terrified. Emma cuddles him, a sweet smile on her face. "Shhh ... shhh," she soothes, "that's my little honey love. Shhh, for Mama."

The baby continues to scream until it seems ready to burst. Emma glares at Jes. A ray of hate. She screams into his face. "GET OUT. JUST GET OUT."

Jes stumbles back against the wall in confusion, watching her, as if in a dream. Rocking the baby gently in her arms, Emma croons softly. "Shhh ... shhh. My little love dove." But the baby continues to screech, deaf to everything but his own fear. Emma, losing her patience, shakes him violently and rushes from the room shouting. "OH, SHUT UP. FOR FUCK SAKE, SHUT UP!"

Jes, momentarily paralyzed with anger, listens to her clomping down to the kitchen.

The baby's shrieks, mingled with Emma's roars, tumble back up to him. He draws in a deep breath to calm his rage and the smell of gas stings his nostrils. In two leaps he is down the stairs.

Emma is holding the baby over the hissing gas cooker "Just a little whiff," she sings, "just a little whiff, my honey love. To make mamma's baby sleep ... Shhh!"

Jes lunges forward and snaps off the gas ring. Grabbing Emma and the baby he drags them out of the kitchen into the fresh air.

. . .

'Mother's' sitting room is festooned with brassy gee-gaws. She sits in

their midst enveloped in her cavernous armchair. Jes stands awkwardly inside the door. There is no invitation to sit.

'Mother' sucks in smoke and snorts through her nostrils. "What diya want?"

Jes picks nervously at a nail. "After she had the baby," he begins. "She - she hasn't been the same. She's taking that stuff. It's cracking her up. She's ... "

'Mother' shorts, glares at Jes as if at a weed, safe in her knowledge that when the time comes ... Pluck ... Snap!

Jes continues. "She doesn't relate. Not to me anymore. Not to the baby. Not to anything. It's ..."

"Keep yer nose out of it, son. I told you before. It's none a your business." She inhales. Blows. Waves him away. "Now get out."

Jes hesitates, spreading his hands helplessly in supplication, but he can see *'Mother'* is already preoccupied with other thoughts.

As he lets himself out he hears her calling, "Sonny!" Stopping momentarily, thinking he is being recalled, Jes glimpses the dark shadow of 'Sonny' slipping across the hallway behind him into *'Mother's'* room.

When Jes returns home the sweet smell of gas still lingers in the room. Emma is balled up on the bed with the baby cradled to her breast.

Jes shakes her gently. "Wake up, Emma. Wake up."

Emma does not respond. Taking her arm, Jes tries to pull her to her feet, but Emma resists, waving her hand in slow motion to brush him aside.

"Go away," she mumbles.

He shakes her again. "Emma!"

No response.

Jes reaches for the child and gently prizes him away from her. The baby breathes peacefully through his perfect button nose. The smell of baby shit and gas mingle in Jes's nostrils as he carries him quietly to the bedroom door.

Without warning, Emma springs at him, her eyes wild and fierce. "I TOLD YOU BEFORE," she snarls clawing the infant from him, "GIMME MY BABY." Hurling herself and the child back on the bed she wraps herself protectively around him again.

. . .

Jes sits at the bar cradling a mug of coffee between his hands to stop them shaking. Defeated, he aches for a drink, knowing he mustn't. Mustn't cloud his mind. But it is already enveloped in a fog. He sips his coffee dejectedly, unaware of 'Sonny', sitting like a shadow behind him, watching him silently. Jes drains his coffee and heads through the door, across the yard, to the toilets.

As he unzips, a savage pain shears through the back of his neck. He stumbles to the floor, gasping as another torrent of blows rain on him. Smashing his ribs. Tearing his face. Crushing his genitals.

From above him he hears a thin rasping voice.

"A present from *'Mother',*" it snarls. "Sweet dreams."

In the nothingness, as if from the end of a long tunnel, children are singing a familiar skipping song ...

"Kiss the Wizard once / Kiss the Wizard twice / Kiss the Wizard three times and you shout /

Kiss the Wizard four / Kiss the Wizard five / Kiss the Wizard six times and you're OUT."

As his mind blacks and blanks his final thought is for the cool safe sanctuary of the ash tree.

THE SQUATTER

A thought that Colm had not had for some time had, just now, flashed into his mind. It wasn't a pleasant thought and try as he might he couldn't dislodge it. The more he attempted to brush it away the stronger the image became, playing over and over like a looped film clip, on the frontal screen of his mind.

He attempted to recall where the thought had come from, hoping that if he could pin down its source, he might be able to dig it up like an old root and discard it on his mental rubbish tip - like the trash facility on his computer. Pick it up, drop it in, delete it.

But it wasn't that simple. His brain, he knew, was much more complicated than his computer. By pressing a button or key he had total control over the machine - a facility not available with the human brain which had to deal with the added complications of feelings, emotions and associations.

Colm pictured an imaginary mechanical digger dredging though the layers of his thoughts, scooping up this one, then that one, and dumping them onto the banks of his memory as if from a dump or the levels in an archaeological dig. The digger had dredged up this particular hideous image, as if at random, exposing it for his attention.

Here, have a look at this. I found it buried away down in your brain. Pretty gruesome, isn't it?

It was. And once presented with it Colm found he was unable to stop examining the thought in all its gory detail. It would not go away.

Colm, quick to jump to his own defense, reminded himself that his thoughts were not always so random. Mostly, he was in control. Only sometimes, at a moment like this, when he was sitting daydreaming into the fire, a random thought like this one leapt from the depths and stared him straight in the eye.

On this drizzly Sunday afternoon, with Laura engrossed in a book beside him, paying him no attention, he fought the intruder in his mind.

It's all very well when the thought is pleasant, he brooded, but not when, as now, the specimen is particularly ugly.

He shifted uneasily on the couch as if to shoo it away before Laura noticed his discomfort. He wanted to slip quickly and comfortably into his previous state of reverie where enjoyable thoughts flowed like endless streams of ticker-tape. But he couldn't. The present image refused to budge. It's talons dug into his consciousness and perched there, like a leering gremlin, refusing to leave.

Even as his tongue began to formulate a description of it, to tell Laura, another part of his mind pounced, clamped down on it, stopping him. All in that split second when the signals of speech were being delegated to his tongue.

Just in the nick of time too, he decided, because it would have shocked her.

His face, he realized was screwed up like a ball of paper as if he had a filthy object in his mouth. This, he chuckled to himself, is interesting. The urge to spit is appropriate too because the thought has to do with taste and something nasty. *Aach*! Nasty isn't the word for it. *Contemptible! Foul! Despicable!* But even these descriptions aren't satisfactory. The urge to cough it up and spit it out is acute. But he can't.

Turning his head away from Laura, he feigns interest in a picture on the wall - one he is very fond of - to divert his attention. It was no use. Because he had stopped the image flying out of his mouth in the form of words it now seemed to have attached itself to him in a hovering, taunting, image. Why and from where had it cropped up again? Maybe it was something he had read somewhere or been told. Anyway, it wasn't the kind of thing one could recount to one's girlfriend - or anybody else for that matter. But *dammit,* somehow he had acquired it and, like it or not, the thing was deposited in his memory bank. It surfaced now with the urgency of a bad cheque.

Colm rummaged through the memory files in his mind for a new idea. One that was strong enough to knock the squatting gremlin off it's perch and shatter it to smithereens. Nothing surfaced apart from trivia that wasn't strong enough to sustain itself let alone banish the sturdy intruder.

The damn thing grew in stature, dressed in it's awful finery, lurching and leering at him, calcifying itself on an inner pedestal from where it dripped over and down like a ghoul in some horror movie.

He spoke suddenly, anything, to distract himself. "D'you know, since the motor car was invented it has been responsible for over thirty million deaths? Amazing, huh? I heard it on the radio last night. Some professor. A lecture on the environment..."

Laura looked up from her book and gazed at him for some seconds, her thoughts miles away in her novel, her eyes focused somewhere behind him. He repeated himself. Her eyes came slowly into focus.

"Oh," she said with a dismissive shrug of her shoulder and slid back into her reading.

He watched as her attention settled once more into the depths of her book.

Now I'm in trouble, he thought. I've failed to engage her attention or to dislodge this damn gremlin.

Laura reached out without looking up and laid a hand on his arm. "Huhn, you all right?" she mumbled.

Colm knew she wasn't really interested in an answer but was simply letting him know that, for her, he did exist. But, for now, it was on the periphery of her consciousness. Laura abruptly snapped the book shut, stretched, and sprang from the couch. "Cup of tea?" she asked over her shoulder as she headed for the kitchen.

Colm didn't reply. Annoyed at the suddenness of her leaving he swiveled around in his seat while watching her in disparagement.

"You want some tea?" Laura called again. Water, splashing from tap to kettle, drowned out any answer he might have made. He waited for the noise to abate before replying.

"Yes, please," he said, loudly, with just a hint of protest.

I want your full attention. You're not giving it to me. There's something on my mind. I can't tell you because it would horrify you to hear it and embarrass me to say it.

His tone brought Laura to the kitchen doorway. She stopped to study him; head cocked to one side, lips held tight, eyes darting about his face as if to speed-read it.

They scrutinized each other for a few seconds. She's trying to read my thoughts, Colm realized, and I'm trying to read hers.

Laura's expression seemed to ask, *Is there something on your mind that you want to tell me? You look upset. I hope it's not what I'm thinking. Sometimes you can be a demanding bastard. Especially when I'm trying to read in peace.*

He watched as her face gave a questioning twitch.

Colm's face answered, *Yes, there is something but it's not what you're thinking at all. There's a bad taste in my mouth from an ugly image in my head but I can't tell you what it is.*

Then a new thought dawned, filling him with wonder and amazement. The muscles on my face, triggered by the hideous image, contorted into a complicated combination of delicate shapes to convey a message more acute, more artful and subtle, than actual words. Laura's face, with its more delicate muscular structure, is answering and questioning my expression at the same time. It's as if our faces have a life of their own, engaged in a silent conversation of facial expressions.

He grinned as the full force of the idea hit him. *Our faces are having a conversation!*

In his excitement Colm completely forgot about the gremlin that, up to a moment ago, had haunted his mind. Unheeded, it tottered, fell off it's perch, and shattered to dust. The squatter was evicted and Colm was completely unaware of it.

THE LIZARD IN THE GLASS JAR

Helen stared at the lizard imprisoned in the glass jar. It stood in the centre of the table directly on a level with her face.

A spiky frill ran down the middle of its back, separating at the base, and continuing on either side of its long tail. Attached to the tip of the creature's tail was a length of rough green string like she had seen her father use to tie up rose bushes in the garden. On the end of this string, which curled around the inside of the jar like a vine, was a large serrated leaf.

Helen could see no join or knot where the string was attached to the lizard or the leaf to the string. It seemed to her as though they were all one entity, furled together in the jar. A thin black forked tongue, flicking in and out of the lizard's mouth at intervals, made Helen squirm nervously.

"Don't be afraid." Her father's mellow tones came from far above her. Helen was glad of his protective presence because she knew she could not stand here on her own with this reptile's little black eyes staring steadily back at her. At the same time she was aware that her father had brought her here for some purpose yet to be revealed. She waited.

Although the lizard showed no expression, beyond its staring, Helen was sure it was unhappy. She felt sorry for it, as she would for any trapped animal, but shunned the idea of ever wanting it for a pet. She was glad that a heavy stopper, securely fixed in the broad neck of the jar, kept this hideous creature locked in its glass prison. She had a strange feeling that this lizard was in some way connected with herself.

"You see the string-like pieces growing out of the leaf," her father said. "You can eat those."

Helen, unable to tear her eyes away from the reptile's hypnotic gaze, pictured her father's thin face smiling above her. She couldn't be sure if he was joking or serious. It was what she called his 'game-playing' smile. But this was a strange game.

Her father continued. "They're very good for you," he said, his voice warm and persuasive. "Actually, they make you big and strong."

She watched in alarm as his large hands, appearing to float from either side of her, reached out and grasped the jar. The lizard stiffened. Helen stiffened too and would have jumped back had her father not been standing close behind her blocking her retreat.

A flutter of panic clutched at the pit of her stomach. Missing the safe contact with his hand made her feel uneasy. Then, as she felt once more his reassuring presence around her, the panic subsided. After all, she reassured herself, it was only a game.

Her father held the jar firmly on the table. His hands are so big and strong, Helen marveled. Hands she saw digging and planting in the garden. Hands that could lift her high in the air. She felt safe until he began to remove the stopper. Sucking in her breath she held it, in dread, unsure of what to do next.

The lizard raised its repulsive head with a jerk and sniffed at the influx of fresh air. Then, abruptly, it scraped its way to the rim of the jar and slithered down onto the table, dragging the string and the leaf in its wake.

Helen shuddered. The game was getting scary now. She stifled a scream and stood fixed to the spot by the sudden agility of the lizard's movement. In the time it had taken her to draw and hold her breath, all was free of the jar. The lizard had stopped, as if knowing instinctively the precise distance to move from its imprisonment to free itself and its attachments, and continued to stare fixedly at her.

Now that the creature was out in the open Helen could see the loose skin below its chin pulsating with the rhythm of it's silent breathing. Her urge was to flee but the table blocked her in front, her father blocked her from behind, his huge arms cut her off left and right. Now she was imprisoned and the lizard was free.

As her father picked up the leaf, holding it in front of her, she saw that the reptile, string, and leaf, were indeed all one. With a gentleness that belied the size of his hands, he plucked a piece of thread-like membrane from the leaf and placed it on the table before her.

“Now, eat that,” he said, “it’ll do you good. Then we’ll go and watch the parade like I promised.”

The lizard made no movement, its eyes fixed on Helen’s, as if waiting to see what she would do.

Her little heart thumped in her breast. She tried to raise her arm to take the piece of leaf as her father had told her, but fear froze her.

What if the lizard disapproved, she thought, at having a little girl eating a part of it? But, she tried to reason, it hadn’t done anything when her father nicked off a piece of its leaf. It lay on the table where her father had placed it, between her and the lizard, crouched exactly where it had stopped, still silently watching her.

Helen released her breath slowly, feeling her father’s hand lift hers and curl her fingers around the little piece of stringy leaf. She didn’t dare look. Her eyes were glued to the lizard’s as she waited for its reaction.

The reptile simply stared back. Helen was afraid to blink.

She became aware of her father’s voice again but now it seemed to be inside her head.

'Eat up fast, the parade will be starting any minute, we don’t want to miss it'. He placed his hands - frightening hands now - on either side of her, palms flat on the table, waiting.

Tentatively Helen picked up the little piece of leaf and held it in front of her between her eyes and the lizard’s. It felt soft and warm in her fingers at first but, as she hesitated, still uncertain, it seemed to lose its softness, growing larger and becoming rigid.

Above her she heard her father's sharp intake of breath and, as he exhaled slowly, it felt like a hot tongue licking the top of her hair.

His sense of urgency penetrated her, as his hands, one pushing her head gently from behind, while the other held her own small hand, guiding it, insistently, with the ever thickening tendon, towards her waiting mouth.